EXTENSION
CLASS

EXTENSION CLASS

The Classic Four

Yvonne Effiong

Extension Class

Copyright © 2020 by Yvonne Effiong. All rights reserved.

No part of this publication may be reproduced, stored in a retrieval system or transmitted in any way by any means, electronic, mechanical, photocopy, recording or otherwise without the prior permission of the author except as provided by USA copyright law.

The opinions expressed by the author are not necessarily those of URLink Print and Media.

1603 Capitol Ave., Suite 310 Cheyenne, Wyoming USA 82001
1-888-980-6523 | admin@urlinkpublishing.com

URLink Print and Media is committed to excellence in the publishing industry.

Book design copyright © 2020 by URLink Print and Media. All rights reserved.

Published in the United States of America
Library of Congress Control Number: 2020917354
ISBN 978-1-64753-470-7 (Paperback)
ISBN 978-1-64753-471-4 (Digital)

17.03.20

CHAPTER ONE

The two doctors had spent some time waiting for the arrival of Barr. Martina Alphonsius Effiong. Of the two doctors, Itoro Fred seemed more uneasy and restless. Her restlessness was not fuelled by boredom or atmospheric inconvenience. Rather, she was unimaginably afraid of the possibility of having Martina indulged herself in a combating analysis of the moral justification of having a man arranged for her, thereby disappointing the eventual evening and consequently blowing up all efforts she already invested to bring Chris Chidozie and Martina together. She never wanted this to happen. Itoro tried all the conversations she knew with her young handsome doctor colleague in order to either cover or erase the aggravating delay and subsequently kill a possible surge of anxiety that may prompt him to ask or think the impossible.

However, when she discovered Chris' unusual severe and relaxed countenance, Itoro became less anxious and spoke in her usual confident tone. She knew she had initiated and written a very hard script, but she resolved to depend entirely on the power of her personal discretion to actualize the pairing strategy between her best friend, Martina Effiong, a young intelligent, humble and chastised lady and Chris Chidozie, a young brilliant outgoing and self-controlled doctor colleague. In her judgment, a good beautiful young woman like Martina who proved the supremacy of her self-dignity even as far back as their secondary school days, deserved to be happy and even more with a disciplined and focused young man like Chris. While Itoro and Chris continued the wait for the female of the evening to arrive, they slowly sucked their drinks from the straws which bridged and transported their drinks from the bottles to their mouths in such a stylish manner that left an impression of a purposeful barricade to prevent any unwanted talk.

As Itoro continued to draw her drink through the straw, she quickly noticed the drink in the bottle could not resist the force which moved through the straw and brought it up through the thin hollow tube to her mouth. She also noticed the force which moved along the thin straw was more powerful than the drinks; hence the liquid could not but follow the greater power. She quickly discovered that if she must successfully pair the intelligent beautiful and dignified Martina with any man, she must brilliantly but diplomatically become the stronger force just to make Martina succumb to the will greater than hers. At this realization, she dialed Martina's number. When the voice at the other end emerged, Itoro's voice spontaneously metamorphosed into a playful teasing until she had an assurance from Martina that she soon will join both of them. Just before the line went off, Martina was heard enquiring whether Brain Etuk, Itoro fiancé would be part of the outing. Itoro answered Martina and quickly gave a justification why Brain would not be present at the meeting.

Itoro, Martina and Brain were so close while still in secondary school few years back. After their Senior School Certificate Examination, their meetings were not as regular as it used to be. By the time they sat for the Joint Admission and Matriculation Examination and finally had admissions into the university to study courses of their designated choices, it became obvious that they three would seldom meet. But when Martina Effiong was admitted into the University of Calabar to study law, while Brian Etuk and Itoro Fred were both admitted into the University of Port Harcourt to study Mechanical Engineering and Medicine respectively, it was so established that it may take personal efforts or ever sheer luck to have Martina's constant company. As predictably envisaged, both Itoro and Brain neither did see nor run into Martina within the time span of seven years. Then on that fateful day, Itoro was paying for items she bought in a supermarket, when a fair beautiful lady calmly walked passed her without looking in her direction. Itoro paused and observed the lady's strides, her composure and the way she carried herself. Just then, she thought within herself that even though she could not see the lady's face, the lady sure had the frame and attracting physique of Martina. By the time she reached the point of conviction, the lady had passed through the access door and concentrated her movement to a point she could board a taxi.

At this point, Itoro made a swift decision which sent her running out towards the lady. Immediately she was at a range of visible closeness, she called out in a tone that prompted Martina's response by turning in a spasm of multiple surprises. When Martina saw Itoro, she was frozen in shock before forcefully releasing herself from her stationary posture. In great excitement, she covered up the very short distance in quick successive strides; jumped on Itoro and screamed in a tone of joyous reconciliation. The two young ladies took some time exchanging pleasantries, admiring each other, making enquiries into oblivious events and making remarks of approval to each other. In the series of question-and-answer session, Itoro told Martina she was doing her housemanship at the National Hospital. Itoro also discovered that Martina was doing her National Youth Service Corps at the National Assembly. Thankful at the providence of reuniting, both ladies exchanged numbers; fixed the next two days for detailed discussions and finally parted with a sense of satisfaction.

Two days later, Itoro and Martina met at the Millennium Park. They correlated their past experiences with the present. There and then, Martina came to a cover that Itoro Fred and Brain Etuk would soon get married. "Oh-o-o!" Martina screamed at the information. "So both of you had a strong touch with each other and hid it all these years? So that seeming closeness with Brain from our secondary school days was not ordinary after all?"

'Not exactly,' Itoro replied. 'Brain you know is a nice guy, but it never crossed my mind we could date until we found ourselves in the same University. Once there, we became very close and before we had time to define what we were into, we saw ourselves seriously in love. The rest of the story is where it has landed us now and this is what we are planning for.'

Martina expressed how glad she was to hear such great tidings. On enquiry, she learnt Brain was working with Ebony Oil Services. Seeking a truth into Martina's personal life and the reality of her dream partner, Itoro shockingly learnt Martina was the same old person who kept her distance from men. She was so disappointed to know that despite Martina's outstanding demeanour and beautiful character, she was still single and had no man in her life at all. Then what even astonished her most was the fact that Martina was neither disturbed that she had no man in her life nor did she make a conscious effort to get herself a man. Out of concern, Itoro told Martina about Chris Chidozie whom she spoke particularly as being so handsome and not indulging. Not initially interested, Martina waved the idea aside. But when Itoro continuously insisted, Martina reluctantly gave her consent to what seemed like Itoro's flowering innovation of the century.

While their conversation continued, Martina told Itoro how she ran into Charlotte Charles.

'Which Charlotte Charles?' Itoro asked in great interest.

'Which other Charlotte Charles do you know? Martina asked rhetorically.

'Charlotte of the "Classic Four"?' Itoro asked keenly.

'Yes of course!' Martina affirmed. 'We met at the Law School nineteen months ago. She never studied medicine again as planned. She said she could not put up with that carefulness and over meticulous attitude of doctors, hence had to reassemble subjects at her Matriculation Exams to introduce herself into a fresh course of study. In fact, we were in the same Law School for three months and never knew it.'

'That sounds great' Itoro said delightfully. 'It means it's possible to meet with all our secondary school contemporaries.'

'Of course, it is,' Martina concurred.

'So what about the rest three of the "Classic Four"? Did you enquire about their whereabouts?' Itoro asked Martina. 'Yes, I did. Charlotte said the four of them were all at the University of Uyo. She said Mmamma Mmenyene got married two years ago, a year before she started her service year. Alice should sure get married by now since Charlotte said her fiancé in England was only waiting for her service year to be over and Becky got married some months back.' Martina said.

'So what about Charlotte herself. Wasn't there a man for her?' Itoro asked.

'Why shouldn't there be?' Martina said rhetorically. 'Of course, there is!'

'So did she ask you whether you were still acting holy just as you used to act and be in our secondary school days? Itoro asked Martina.

'She did,' Martina said. 'She wanted to know whether I was hooked to any man yet.'

'And what did you tell her?' Itoro asked.

'What else? Of course, I told her men who came my way walked away for one reason or the other. I also assured her that mine will stay when he comes no matter the reason that chases other men away,' Martina said.

'Sweetheart, I like your courage. But be rest assured that I won't give up until you meet my young doctor colleague Chris Chidozie. He is just different,' Itoro said.

'Well, he will prove how different he is when I meet him. After all, Charlotte told me all men like to have "show" before fully accepting a woman. She took time to lecture me that men no longer buy packaged goods these days. She said they must unpackage it; touch, feel and experiment it to know how much it is worth. In fact, she said no man gives a damn about virginity!' Martina said. With this, Martina and Itoro burst out in great laughter. After several moment of assessing Charlotte's lecture about men, sex and marriage, both women started laughing all over again. Then Itoro said:

'Charlotte and her three friends were spoilt right from our secondary school days. In fact, the "Classic Four" as a name comes from their deep sense of immorality and even amorality.

As Itoro tapped her left foot continuously against the slippery tiled floor, impatiently looking at her watch and what would become of the rest of the evening, she felt a soft hand rubbing her gently on her back. When she looked up, she saw Martina standing by her side and smiling satisfactorily like a school girl who emerged the best in a competition. Martina was gorgeously appareled in a sharp blue colour that almost reflected the rays from the fluorescent bulb. She wore light cosmetics and had her hair strategically and beautifully packed. Itoro could not help but continuously stared at her. Then with a sudden sense of realization, she showed Martina to a seat before introducing her to Chris and Chris to her. After a short moment of chattering, Itoro excused herself from the company and teasingly encouraged Chris and Martina to have a beautiful time together before setting off apart to their different destinations. As she stood up from her seat, Itoro walked straight to the counter and instructed the attendant to take orders from the sitting duo. After this, she left.

After the departure of Itoro, Chris and Martina spent the rest of the evening discussing themselves. Chris conversation was clothed in genuine pleasantries. He made many mild remarks; fully approved of Martina and also garnished the entire atmosphere with mild jokes. Martina responded to his jokes mildly and conveniently settled herself to enjoy the colour of the atmosphere which was a product of Chris' creation. Their time lasted and fully drew to a close. They exchanged phone numbers, fixed a dinner date for the following week after a detailed discussion and time suitable to both of them and finally zoomed off in Chris' car.

The week following, Chris gave Martina a reminder call. The latter willingly obliged and at exactly 7.30p.m. Chris found his way to Martina's residence. Martina emerged in a pink beautiful floral gown. Chris starred at her and almost lost his balance. He managed to control himself, but not without a visible squirm. After closing the door after Martina, Chris turned to the driver's side, entered the car and drove off. At the restaurant they chose, they both sat at a table they believed would be most convenient for them. Once there, Chris spent almost the first fifty seconds gazing greedily at Martina. When it became apparent to her and she finally turned the attention of her full eyes to look at him, Chris tactfully evaded them and remembered just then that he had not made an order. With the sounds he made with the clip of his finger and thump, he attracted the attention of a waiter who approached them almost the same time. He brought the menu to help both Chris and Martina conveniently determine their choice.

Immediately the waiter got their order, Chris resumed his duty of gazing directly into the face of Martina. This time he did it with boldness that was not subject to any consciousness of being caught. He took his time to examine her eyes, nose, mouth and even ears until Martina became consciously inconvenienced.

'What?' Martina slightly raised alarm, 'You are gazing at me in such an embarrassing way and even gazing outside the bounds of civilization?'

'Really?' Chris replied rhetorically. 'You wouldn't blame me. Your beauty is so tempting; so unique and so rare!'

'Well, I appreciate your approval, compliment or whatever it is classified as,' Martina said. Then added immediately, 'I hope you never did this oratory odd just to specially render it to me?'

With this, both Chris and Martina busted out in spontaneous laughter. At this point, the waiter came with their order.

Immediately he finished serving them and left, Chris lifted up his eyes and had them fixed on Martina before plainly saying:

'Martina, those remarks weren't practiced. They came out of my heart. You are so unique and I knew it instinctively right from the first day I saw you. I want you to know that from the depth of my heart I love you. I so do right from the first time I set my eyes on you.'

'Well,' Martina begun in reply, 'I really have to dispute your claim and may even be tempted to state that it doesn't follow a logical occurrence of event. Take, for example, how great a stranger I am to you. You definitely may not know what you are talking about.' She paused and smiled for a while before saying, 'You barely know who I am and you are already talking about loving me?'

'Why do you possibly think I'm lying? Every human can determine what he wants by just fixing his interest and focus at a time. From the first instance of seeing you, I fell in love with you because I fixed my interest and focus on you,' Chris said.

'Well, what I probably would understand about that is infatuation. Every man has the capacity to misinterpret infatuation for love. Infatuation is every man's interest and focus. However, love in GOD's way is possible; but love in man's way is absolutely impossible; Martina said.

This slightly stunned Chris who sat for a while before gathering his wit together.

'Where did you get that from? Is it from your training as a lawyer?' After a brief moment of contemplation, Chris asked, 'Anyway, tell me more about yourself. Apart from being a Barrister at Law, I want to know who Martina really is. I mean something different?'

'Something different?' Martina asked rhetorically. 'Well, Martina Alphonsius Effiong is a barrister at law as you already know; doing her national assignment at the National Assembly, Legislative Arm. She was born twenty-four years ago to Mr. and Mrs. Alphonsius Effiong of Ikot Akan in Akwa Ibom State. She is the second child in the family of four children – two males and two females. She likes reading and meeting handsome guys like Chris Chidozie. Martina has a son.'

'What?' Chris exclaimed unconsciously.

'What is that? What do you mean?' Martina asked noncommittally.

'Sorry–I mean... I mean that was so impressing. But the part I don't quite understand is the son thing. Are you serious or you are just kidding me?' Chris said after an initial moment of stammering.

'Kidding you? Why? What for? How can I joke about a thing like that? I have a son. I mean it and that is the reality of it all' Martina declared.

The revelation stunned Chris and forced him into an unplanned withdrawal. A sudden silence was introduced into the atmosphere and it seemed that euphoria of flirty comments unexpected disappeared. The weight of the comment reflected on the face of Chris. He could not help but unconsciously demonstrate the impact of the revelation and the series of disappointment that assembled on his entire body. All the while he was struggling to come to terms with the reality that Martina was not what he thought her to be, the full unblinking eyes of Martina were fixed on him in such great concentration as if her entire life depended on her special observatory session of him. Then

EXTENSION CLASS

he seemed to be conscious of his surroundings and the steady gaze, but not as manly as he did when they first came into the restaurant. Gradually, his gaze became fixed on her.

'Now what?' Martina said slightly amused. 'You are so disappointed? Probably you will walk away like others at the mention of my past of cankerworm. You see why it is complete error to love when you know nothing about a person? You see, where reality starts, interest and focus end there!'

'No, no, no,' Chris begun, trying to cover up the lapses in his visible reaction,' It's not so. It's just that I'm surprised because you do not look anything like a woman who has given birth.

'How old is he?'

'He is seven; Martina said, producing a portrait of her son from her wallet.

She handed over the portrait to Chris. He received it, took a good view of the boy's image and looked back at Martina.

'He's so cute,' Chris forced himself to utter the words.

'Yea, he is. I love him so much; Martina concurred and declared.

'What is his name?' Chris asked.

'Divine! Divine is his name; Martina said enthusiastically.

Chris continued staring at Divine's image jealously and absentmindedly.

'What are you thinking about? Or is it that you don't like my son?' Martina deliberately asked Chris.

'Me'? Chris asked in a sudden reawakening. 'Of course, I like him a lot!'

With that, he forced a smile and handed back the portrait to Martina. Not able to continue the conversation, Chris tactfully called the dinner to a close. Trying to cover the state of his emotions, he asked whether Martina had fun.

'Yes of course I did. Thanks so much for the dinner,' Martina replied.

'I'm glad you did,' Chris said, forcing out a courtesy.

When Chris had dropped off Martina and sped off, she sat alone so disappointed at Chris reaction to the information she gave him. She thought how he couldn't even say he loves her again after the disclosure. She knew the problem with men was their disposition towards young single mothers who still needed husbands of their own despite their unfortunate past. Martina was not unaware how they treated single mothers like the deadliest plague. Although it was an unfortunate situation, she couldn't nurse the thought that a man would come in-between her and her son, Divine. Even though Chris was the fourth man who had walked out of her life because of the knowledge that she had given birth to a son, she was determined that any man who loved her enough to accept her as wife must first accept her son. This was a resolution and nothing would break it.

Immediately Chris got to the office the next morning, he went straight to Itoro. He asked her to see him just outside the theatre. He did not stand out there up to seventy seconds when Itoro joined him. She was so disappointed to discover how sour his countenance was. She enquired about his outing with Martina and he affirmed its success. Itoro made several other enquiries to get details or the source of Chris' sullen mood, but he did not utter any word. She continued asking and even suggested Martina as the source of his morose temper, but Chris continued in silence while one of his feet made indiscriminate drawings on the ground. Exhausted with Chris unyielding silence, Itoro threatened to walk away. Just then, Chris' voice emerged in artificial humility.

'Ity, you said Tina is your best friend and you guys were in the same high school?'

'Yes, I did say so,' Itoro replied with eyes of expectation.

'Then in that case you should know more than enough about her?' Chris said.

'Of course, I certainly know so much about her. If I didn't, I wouldn't have introduced you to her,' Itoro said.

'That is my point,' Chris said. 'You didn't tell me she was a third-rate and a second-hand girl!'

'I beg your pardon!' Itoro said, almost yelling.

'You heard me right. You didn't tell me she is a mother of a seven year old son? You would have told me she had a baby during high school!'

'You are dreaming Chris! This is quite unbelievable. You dare not say such thing about my friend! What baby? In which high school? In fact, what are you talking about? This whole thing sounds so ridiculous'.

'I'm not dreaming; neither am I being ridiculous. In fact, it is so believable. Martina told me herself and even showed me the photograph of her son Divine?' Chris said.

'Divine? Who is Divine?' Itoro asked.

The story sounded very strange to Itoro. She was so confused.

How on earth could Martina have a son and she was not aware. She doubted the entire make-up of the story. She neither could affirm nor discard the story, hence decided to find out the true arrangement of things and how Martina wanted either the real or the ideal to occur in her universe. She assured Chris everything would be fine and that she would get back to him immediately she verified the matter herself.

Few days later, Itoro visited Martina with an intention to clarify the state of things; stabilize her mind with the truth of the Divine-story and reconcile herself with Martina's complexity that was both unique and bizarre. In front of Martina's door, she rang the doorbell twice before pressing the knob of the door downwards to gain entrance into the house almost simultaneously. Inside the house, Martina was busy perusing a big encyclopedia-like book on whose cover leaf was written: Complication of the Evolving Constitution of Nigeria since Frederick Lugard. She heard the ringing of the doorbell and the opening of the door and stood up fully alert. When she got to the foyer and discovered it was Itoro, she relaxed again. As Martina picked up the massive book and returned to her formal position, she began to tease Itoro who deliberately ignored and followed her.

Now duly seated, she continued teasing Itoro who continued looking at her without a word. Then Martina asked Itoro why she was so quiet since she would not be without any reason. Martina insisted on the reason for the unusual silence because she knew Itoro would not be silent without a cause. Just then, Itoro seized the opportunity to tell Martina how she thought she knew Martina too well since they have been best of friends from secondary school, only to discover that

Martina kept away sensitive issues from her. Itoro's playful sharp tone stunned Martina. Then fully taken aback that Chris must have told her about the breaking news of the fact she has a son, she deliberately trivialized Itoro's accusation by feigning to know nothing about it. Itoro continued to insinuate and finally mentioned what Chris told her of she having a son. Martina laughed it off and tactfully scolded Itoro for putting up such a serious and sullen appearance for a matter that was so minute and insignificant. Then Martina asked Itoro to shake off her serious mood so they both can talk about serious matters. Her friend rejected her sardonic request and insisted hearing everything that transpired between her and Chris in their outing, not excluding the sudden new development which was both strange and shocking. When Martina neither rejected nor confirmed the true state of things, Itoro pacified the atmosphere and took a seat close to Martina to get the truth, using sympathetic grounds.

'Come on Tina,' Itoro began pleadingly,' you know it's not true. Why did you have to lie to him? He's so upset.'

'Lie about what? Martina asked in serious tone.

'About you having a son,' Itoro replied.

'Who told you it's a lie? Why should I lie about such a thing?' Martina said rhetorically.

The question made Itoro laugh for a while before saying.

'Tell me you're joking. Just tell me it's one of your expensive jokes to scare men away from you,' Itoro said.

'I'm not joking, Doctor Itoro Fred,' Martina said in an emphatically serious voice.

'Divine is my son and I can't joke about this!'

The truth of the matter left Itoro very stunned. She sat, speechlessly looking at Martina. She seemed not to recover for hundreds of seconds. The information left a great impression on her which could not be described.

When the moments of her shock was over, Itoro spent time making enquiries of Divine's father, the time Martina took in without anyone's knowledge; how she managed the period of her pregnancy and how the man who got her pregnant won her heart. Martina evaded Itoro's questions and the latter accused her of being too secretive. Immediately Itoro accused her, Martina seized the opportunity to also accuse Itoro of falling in love with Brain without telling her, all with the intention of totally killing the story of Divine's birth.

'That I have a child in not enough reason for Chris to behave that way,' Martina said, completely diverting.

'He is in love with you. I think he's just confused about what you told him or don't you think it was rather too early for you to have let him know?' Itoro said.

'No, I don't think so,' Martina started in explanation.

'It is better he knows now than later. Suppose we fell in love and he later gets to know, he would be heartbroken. Moreso, if he knows later and walks away, I won't or may not be able to come back to myself.'

'You are right. I will speak to him,' Itoro assured Martina.

'On the contrary, do not try to persuade him. Allow him to his will. I mean let him follow his heart,' Martina admonished.

The two friends spent the rest of the evening in discussions that appealed to their interests until Itoro judged the proper time she would leave Martina's place. When Itoro finally left, Martina returned back to studying the Compilation of the Evolving Constitution of Nigeria since Frederick Lugard.

The following morning was somewhat wet from a slight drizzle. Itoro met Chris at the hospital. He was slightly sullen and very serious with his work. After a little while, he walked up to Itoro to find out whether she had seen Martina. Itoro affirmed his question and he seemed desperate to know whether the issue of Martina having a son was true. Itoro maintained her ground of uncertainty and finally asked how much Chris loved Martina not to be able to overlook the presence of a son. Chris stood for sometime in deep thought and slowly nodded the possibility of overlooking Martina's son, but instead looking firmly at the extent to which he loved her. Just then, he remembered he had neither spoken nor seen Martina since the last outing.

Chris stayed for another two weeks before putting a call through to her. On the other end, Martina saw his call and ignored it. He tried other times and witnessed similar results. Then that evening, she had just finished shopping and picking some food items from a grocery store when a text from Chris alerted her. She looked at it and also ignored it. Two hours later, while she was trying to get herself a quick meal, she discovered someone was both impatiently ringing her doorbell and banging her door in slightly heavy fist. When she summoned courage to open up, she was beyond measure astonished to see Chris in front of it. In feigned lack of interest, she enquired why he would visit her place without first informing her. He defended how he had tried to reach her without success. In conviction that Chris was dead serious to see her, Martina bade him come into the house. He did and made himself comfortable. After a brief excuse, Martina went into the kitchen to fix dinner for both of them. When she was done, she brought a dish and everything necessary for two. They both sat on the floor and had the dinner together.

After the dinner, Chris knelt and apologized and Martina acknowledged his apology. With the air rid of suspicion and dirty secrets, Chris and Martina begun dating. But no relationship started without Martina taking out a good time to intimate Chris how no act of pre-marital sex would be accommodated without a recognizable ground to encourage the act. In other words, she made herself clear that no act of sex in whatever classification would be tolerated before marriage. Chris accepted the conditions, though in passive eagerness. However, their relationship was filled with colour. They would go to places together and somewhat had glimpse of each other's schedules. Then they would go to movies, club, go to any museum park; spend time in outing and walking out a conscious strategy for eventful fun after their hectic moments at work.

A month after the relationship begun, Martina completed her assignment with the National Youth Service corps and formally did her passing out. The party for the celebration held at Chris' place. Martina, Chris and Itoro were the major participants. The atmosphere was charged with an aura that was so colourful and inviting. The sequences of the music that flowed out of the large home theatre immersed the trio in an enjoyable moment and induced them into some innovative dance steps. Then they took turns in drinking and having their meals. Not long, Itoro left. Martina and Chris spent the rest of the evening enjoying themselves.

The atmosphere was still the same – the atmosphere of intense feeling, tempting both Chris and Martina with a passionate desire to go down the impenetrable. As the music continued, they both unconsciously move closer and closer to each other until they unconsciously grabbed themselves, engaged the power of a kiss that had dwelt in their sub-consciousness for as long as they had been thinking of escaping the reality of this aspect that proved unavoidable. Their moment of kiss lasted very deep, passionate and very sensual. Then Chris went down the path of action by stretching himself to undress Martina. When he found the exposed part of her body, he gently caressed it until it was almost becoming a momentary culture. Martina continued to enjoy the sensations that emerged out of Chris commitment until she became conscious that Chris had gone so much out of the positions of his boundaries. She became conscious that Chris' hand was greatly but gently scrubbing her breast in that manly sensuality to the point that she knew she had to stop him immediately or endure the burden of her carelessness and guilt for the rest of her life. Just then, she cut off the pleasure and immediately stopped Chris. Although Martina was discreet in reminding him of the promise to keep out this part of the intimacy, but the whole action greatly disappointed Chris. He made a justification that since they both would get married in the immediate future, it was necessary they had a good feel and fill of each other. But Martina objected, pointing out the correction and great difference which exists between planning to get married and being already married. She went further to tell him that since they had already agreed to keep this part of the deal till after marriage, they had only one option of just doing exactly what they had endorsed.

Then the deal became unexplainable to Chris who suddenly considered it unreasonable for a young lady who had already given birth to a son to still talk about sex after marriage. Then in his moving emotion and the contemplation of reason, these words escaped his mouth:

'What is the stress about sex after marriage? It's not as if you are a virgin. What's all the stress anyway?'

'I knew this would happen. I always knew you will say this to me' Martina said, greatly annoyed. 'Well, go ahead and throw my shame on my face. I don't blame you. I did the mistake for washing my dirty linen before you and of course, you now have every right to ridicule me!'

With that, Martina stormed out of the house. Chris was apologetic. He rushed out of the house after Martina.

'Honey, please I'm really sorry, I didn't mean to say that.'

'Of course, you didn't mean to, but you have said it all the same. Well, what difference will it make? You can never see me the other way. It will always be this way. In fact, I don't think there is any need for you to apologize. This is a warning sign I should not ignore and come to think of it; you are not to blame since I brought myself to your house, trust me, I know exactly what to do; Martina said.

As she boarded a cab, Chris continued to beg that she returns to the house. But while this went on, Martina ordered the cab to zoom off.

Chris continued calling Martina, but she continued rejecting his calls. She deliberately avoided him for few days. Then tired of being ignored, Chris checked out a time he knew Martina would be at home. After ringing the door bell over and over again, Martina reluctantly attended to it. When she discovered it was Chris, she left the door ajar and walked away. Inside the house, Chris tried everything to make Martina accept his apology.

'Honey, I said I'm sorry. You're taking this thing too far. Those words slipped out of my throat and I'm so sorry for being callous. I promise it will never happen again. Believe me, sex can wait. Please forgive me.'

'They slipped out of your throat and you're sorry? How does it sound to you? What makes you sure they will never slip out of your mouth again in even worse manner. I don't think it will work between both of us. So we can give up the whole idea of trying to make something unpleasant pleasant', Martina said.

Chris was unrelenting. He continued begging Martina until Martina assured him she had forgiven him.

A week later, Martina completed her plans to return from Abuja to Uyo. Chris discussed their marriage plans, but Martina insisted he must first go to service and return since he was almost concluding his housemanship. Chris told Martina why he wanted their wedding to take place even before he leaves for the National Youth Service Corps. To terminate the trivial argument, Martina simply told Chris she wanted him to be sure of the kind of woman he wanted, instead of being coerced into a relationship based on his present emotions. Chris tried to persuade Martina into conviction, but discovered she had taken her stand and gave up his persistence.

Two days to the time Martina was to leave for Uyo, Chris took her on outing. While they were still having fun together, Chris asked her:

'So how many children will we have?'

'Two or three maybe. Four is not too much; Martina said.

'Why? What do you mean?' Chris asked.

'Well, what I mean is: we either have two more children in addition to Divine. Or we can have three more children in addition to Divine and we'll have four; Martina explained.

As sudden as Martina mentioned Divine, Chris countenance went completely sour. He withdrew as quickly as he could and despite the conversation Martina tried to initiate, he remained quiet. After few moments of withdrawal, Chris reluctantly asked Martina where Divine was. Martina told him he was with her grandmother. Then he asked again:

'So you intend bringing him along with us?'

'Of course, he's my son and he stays where I stay,' Martina said bluntly.

'But he's not my son, I think he will be better off with your grandmother or you take him to his father,' Chris said in sullen mood.

Martina suddenly went angry. She breathed heavily as she turned fully to face Chris.

'What is the meaning of what you have just said? Are you saying you cannot accept my son if you marry me,' Martina reprimanded.

'No! Don't misunderstand me. That is not what I'm talking about. I was just trying to be factual,' Chris defended.

'Well, factual or not. I can see that this whole thing will not work between us. The reality is I'll not enjoy my marriage with you, because I will spend my entire life, trying to convince you to accept my son. And that is a job I'm not willing to do. There is no point considering marriage when basic visible things cannot be reconciled. I think it's only proper we end this whole thing here before it is late. There is no point considering marriage with you. A man who will not and cannot willingly happily accept my son can never be my husband, Martina declared.

With that, Martina called off the outing and told Chris she was leaving. Chris knew she would not be appeased at that moment so he took her home.

The following day, as usual, Chris tried to sort out issue with Martina. But she insisted not to go back on her decision since the gap between them is wide. Then Chris assured her how he would do anything to make her happy, provided she reconsidered her stand.

'You're ready to do anything to make me happy? What about yourself? Will you be happy doing those things to make me happy or you will just do them to impress me while you are unhappy in your closet,' Martina said, trying to be as logical as possible.

'Honey, I'm ready to sacrifice my happiness for you. Just come back and reconsider your stand,' Chris said desperately.

'Well, I won't accept that. Your happiness will matter a lot in our marriage and I don't intend to diminish it. When you are not happy in a life time thing like marriage, then you are inviting in divorce. I don't want this to happen and cannot be part of this. When we get married and vital issues like the one we had are not resolved, then we certainly are heading to a rock. We cannot rush into marriage and rush out at the same time. This becomes inappropriate to whom we are. I can carry my cross and I don't want you to give it a try,' Martina concluded.

Then Chris told Martina how much he loves her. Martina simply replied that if he loved her that much, he would also love her son, Divine. Since she would leave Abuja for Uyo very early next morning, she politely ended the conversation, retired to her bed so she could be awake early.

While she sat on the chair thinking of her break-up with Chris, she heard a knock on the door. She checked her wristwatch and discovered it was about twenty-five minutes to eleven o'clock. Contemplating who it was, she called out and heard Itoro's voice. She opened up and Itoro came narrating her ordeal with traffic. She had come to assist Martina with packing. But Martina had finished her arrangement and was only waiting for dawn so she could start her journey. Itoro relaxed and made enquiries into other issues and was so astonished to learn that Martina had broken up her engagement with Chris. Itoro had little to say when Martina explained the whole controversy surrounding the issue of her son.

Around 6.00 am the next morning, Itoro and Martina came out with luggage and other traveler's belongings. As they stepped out of the house, a taxi stopped in front of them. A man came out of it. It was Chris Chidozie. He went straight to them. He greeted Itoro and stood in front of Martina. They stared at each other for some time before whispering greetings in low tones.

Chris produced a packaged gift to Martina who received it almost letting tears trickle down her cheek. She handed the gift to Itoro and embraced Chris. Thereafter, she brought out a parcel and handed it over to him. They stood again, looking into each other's eyes in a transcendental admiration. Then they held themselves and passionately went into a rite of kiss. They kissed deeply and intimately until they knew they had their fill. Then Chris ushered Martina into the waiting taxi. Itoro sat at the front, while Martina and Chris sat at the back. At the park, Martina sat by the bus' window. Itoro bade her farewell, but Chris refused to let go. He stood whispering in low tones how he felt about Martina until the bus drove out. They bade each other farewell. Tears crowded the eyes of Martina and Chris struggled not to let his own trickle down. As the bus left his sight, Chris all of a sudden discovered how empty he seemed to be without Martina. This was a reality and he knew he would live with this for a pretty long time.

CHAPTER TWO

Mmamma Teddy Anieboanam was so devastated. Her grief was so immense and her sorrows covered her like the great rivers which ran perpetually deep and infinite. She cried and cried and almost cried out blood. The pains she felt were so unbearable. She could not explain why her entire world was crumbling and worse still, her husband had no glimpse into the situation of things that brought them so much darkness and tears and sweat from her body through the intense pressure of disappointments and black pains that would not leave her alone, her husband stood by her, feeling the deep agony she carried and consoling her. Teddy spent all the energy he had to console his wife Mmamma, but instead her grief persisted.

This was the sixth time Mmamma had a miscarriage. Since her marriage to Teddy, she had not been able to produce a single issue. All the pregnancy GOD blessed her with would simply not stay in her womb. It seemed her womb carried thousands of thorns that choked out the babies in her. In almost twenty years of marriage, each pregnancy terminated itself in its seventh month. The circumstances preceding their termination were usually strange and even disheartening. Then the reality of the steady procession of age towards menopause would set Mmamma on a perpetual fire. Her mother would travel all the way from the country side to console her daughter only for her to join her sorrowful daughter in the rite of tears-breading. Then Teddy would drain off his energy to console both mother and daughter. The fact that Mmamma could not give birth to children despite years of intermittent pregnancies and miscarriages was not really an issue to Teddy.

Teddy was such a complete demonstration of understanding and gentleness. He loved Mmamma and despite all the accusations that he must have been responsible for the ordeals of his wife, he never withdrew his patience. What made Mmamma even more miserable was the rare demonstration of love her husband showed her; hence she perpetually felt the sharp cutting of guilt all over her inward person about her inability to make him a proud father. She was so unhappy and sore displeased with herself that she never gave her husband the least opportunity to show at least a child of his own a love a good father would show his child. Then when she learnt how gossips went round the entire neighbourhood that her husband may afterall be a ritualist who used all his unborn babies for his future wealth, Mmamma locked herself for days weeping and wailing out the misfortunes her incapability permitted her dear and beloved husband to suffer. In fact, for Mmamma Teddy Anieboanam, her hours, weeks and years were embellished and planned out in grief.

Then it became even deadly when her family doctor explained over and over again that she is so normal to carry even triplets in her womb since the wall around her womb is firm. Mmamma would stay awake alone to consistently think out her sanity why she would not carry a child up to nine months and successfully give birth to him. Her situation was a great concern to everyone around her including her mother-in-law. Teddy's mother had tried without success for years to remedy the predicament of her daughter-in-law. But when she could no longer bear the stigma of her daughter-in-law's un-productivity, she resorted to pressurizing her son to get a woman outside matrimony, get her pregnant and keep the name of their family line alive. But her son bluntly refused the suggestion, describing it as a betrayal to the sanctity of marriage. In frustration, Teddy's mother became even more anxious and decided to take up the case from any dimension it requires.

Then as the days, weeks and years went by, Mmamma started to have series of nightmares. Most of the nightmares were children who abused and booed her. They would either chase her away in their thousands or would run away in great fright whenever she approaches them in outstretched hands like a hostess who was begging unwilling guests to honour her invitation. Each of the dreams would push her to wake up immediately. Each time she was woken up by such unusual un-acceptance by the image of what she really wanted, she would spend a great time weeping and reciting all the different names of GOD in an atmosphere of grief she unconsciously created for herself. It was so terrible that Teddy spent almost every night consoling his wife and saying all the words in the world he remembered and which he believed would sooth Mmamma and act as emotional palliatives. Then one day, Mmamma saw a very beautiful child in her womb whom she envisaged and really hoped would be born. Then all of a sudden, her labour started. As she was about being admitted in the labour ward, the unborn child started screaming how he never wanted to be given birth to by Mmamma and requested a doctor who stood by to pull him out of Mmamma's womb immediately. Then the doctor asked him why he preferred leaving, rather than be born and enjoy the care and love Mmamma would show him, he replied that Mmamma was not worthy to have him or any of his brothers. When the doctor refused to pull him out the baby simply metamorphosed into a great mass of blood. Then Mmamma jumped out of the bed in great screams and frightful shrills.

The shrill of Mmamma woke Teddy up. He was also very frightened by the intensity of his wife's screams. Then he began his usual rite of consoling her. But the atmosphere of this particular night looked so eerie. When Teddy looked into his wife's wide-opened and unmovable eyes, all he could hear himself whisper was, 'Jesus! Jesus! Jesus, help my wife! 'Jesus, help me!' He whispered this continuously until the minutes metamorphosed into hours and then slowly, his hands became feeble and dropped down from his wife's shoulder who was now so speechless with an immovable posture. Gradually, the power of sleep held him bound until he nodded to every direction available for his head to exercise his freewill. Slowly, Teddy unconsciously fell on the bed again and rolled in peace to comfortable regions on the foam. But Mmamma never had such an opportunity to exercise her peace the way she could and deem fit. She was restless, worried and uncomfortable all through the night. Then her thought slowly shifted to Charlotte, Becky and Alice. She imagined whether this agony was peculiar to the former well-known 'Classic Four' or it was peculiar to just her. What the next nightmare would be, she could not tell.

Rebecca nearly hit her mother-in-law with her fist if not for the conscious resolutions she made not to engage herself in the endless strives her mother-in-law deliberately invented to make her perpetually depressed. She had been through serious hell in the hands of her in-laws who seemed to enjoy all the pains they caused her for not showing the evidences of her womanhood in the institution of marriage. Not a single woman on earth who believes in the totality of marital relationship would deliberately bar herself from showing the fruit of the womb. It was so unimaginable, especially in a child-conscious society like Africa.

Today, Rebecca's mother-in-law came for nothing but to initiate a fresh provocation which would accord her the great opportunity to make Rebecca recognize once and for all that she is a fourth-class woman who was no different from her husband. How can two men live in the same house in the pretense of love and marriage, Mrs. Ekerette, Rebecca's mother-in-law had asked her on different occasions when she visited her son's house to enforce the reality of the un-idealistic childless marriage.

Rebecca was still enjoying the comic entertaining movie when her mother-in-law suddenly banged the sitting room door, forcefully pushed it and entered unannounced like robbers on a mission to kill their victims and make away with a discovered gold. Immediately she entered the house, her antagonism burst out against Rebecca who was not prepared for such an unexpected scene. She matched straight in great annoyance to the sofa Rebecca reposed, watching her movie and collected the remote from her. She quickly put off the television and begun to question the right her daughter-in-law had to even watch any programme when she ought to use her entire time mourning the shame of inability to give birth to children. Rebecca avoided her for a while, but it seemed the more Rebecca kept silent over the unwarranted confrontation, the more Mrs. Ekerette's temper went sour. Then Rebecca defended herself against all the strange accusations her mother-in-law blurted out to her. But her defense never placated the angry woman who wanted her to give birth immediately. Mrs. Ekerette went angrier and her voice reached the zenith of her strength. She screamed and screamed how inhumanly wicked Rebecca was to continuously give birth to dead children and ceased trying the last four years, thereby attempting to thwart her son's opportunity of being a father and her own chances of becoming a grandmother. She ranted and ranted until Rebecca discovered for the first time that not having a child in a marital home was worse a crime than a well thought-out murder.

Then Rebecca made to walk out of the scene to ameliorate the tantrum of her mother-in-law, but the elderly woman rushed to her and nearly slapped her out for attempting to walk out on her when she was still giving her a recent model of how to have an unwilling daughter-in-law give birth to a living child even when it was outside her strategy for a successful marriage. So Rebecca only stood, listening to all the hard words and abusive language her mother-in-law poured on her. When it was too much for her to bear, a deluge of tears burst out of her eyes and she heard her own voice go out in sudden wails and lamentation. She fell on the floor, cried and cried until she felt a sharp sensation moving across her belly.

Becky, as she was fondly called could not bring herself to think her marriage with Kokoette Attah Ekerette would turn out to be something of ridicule and great sorrow. For the many years that passed and for all the periods she had a great construction of the kind of happiness that will characterize her marriage, never did she envisage terrible ordeals in child-birth as she was experiencing. She did not know where it came from and never even had a time she could reflect and ponder whether nemesis was playing out its law on her. In fact, Becky believed all the still-births she had witnessed were all coincidence, hence there was certainly going to be a time she would have a luck that would outshine her misfortunes. To give herself rest from the harsh reality of four consecutive still-births, she had to avoid getting pregnant for the years that followed. For four years, she stayed avoiding pregnancy and for four years, her in-laws continuously made life so terrible for her.

Despite those turbulent times, Kokoette stood by her and remained a loving husband. Even though her in-laws saw her simply abrasive and proud because she refused to continually brood for not giving birth to a live child, her husband always defended and stood by her. For being that understanding, Becky could relax and trust in her husband's judgment. No man is afraid of war when he has a good weapon to defend him. So seeing Kokoette as her continuous defender, Becky became carefree for another four years and completely forgot how conscious her society was about the relationship between marriage and child-bearing.

Then in the last three months, everything changed. Her loving husband, Kokoette had completely changed and the peace she thought she had secured changed into something of great difficulty and sorrows. Kokoette stopped showing her love and also stopped being so tender. Her presence meant nothing to him and he would talk on phone to women he had affair with in front of Rebecca. Rebecca's world started crumbling. She suddenly became so vulnerable to the attacks of her in-laws. No one was there to defend her.

But despite these recent realities, Rebecca was determined to keep her marriage. She hoped and believed that her beloved husband would come to his senses and continue to be patient with her until GOD visited them with their own live babies. While she consciously kept her will to secure the marriage she so much valued, she never noticed the conspiracy on-going to finally eject her out of her matrimonial home. Then one day, Kokoette opened the door to the sitting room and walked in with a strange lady. The lady followed closely behind. When Becky saw Kokoette walked into the parlour, she stretched out her hands and approached to give him a hug, but Kokoette violently pushed her backwards. She landed on one of the sofas. Just then, she recognized the presence of the strange woman. Then she approached them again to find out who she was and the circumstance that warranted such a hostile attitude from her husband. But everything changed and there was nothing left to seal. Then Rebecca thought about Mmamma, Charlotte and Alice and the negative metamorphosis that suddenly changed the composition of the 'Classic Four' which magnificently remained in control at the time of its popularity.

Nee Charlotte Charles was so distressed that when she entered the hospital for another consultation intended to update her medical status, her countenance and mood were indescribably heavy so that all she was conscious of was the desperation to have a baby. It was so bad that she could recognize nobody nor even acknowledge remarks made by known people. Her heaviness was so unbearable that all that mattered was endless reflections into the enigma that rendered her a pitiable stock for the past eighteen years in the marriage without a single child to show for it.

Charlotte only tested how it felt like for only three months, after which the child died. Hopeful that another pregnancy would come, but for good eighteen years all efforts to conceive a child proved so unnatural and outrageously difficult for Charlotte. Then it became even more unnatural that the same woman who carried a child for nine months gave birth and succored him had suddenly become barren. The first year passed; the second and the third without nothing to show for it. But when it reached the fifth, tenth and fifteenth year, it dawned on Charotte that her battle was something both unknown and unseen. She had had all kinds of medical tests; gone to all best doctors for medical consultations and sought their professional opinions, but all had tuned out unproductive. Then she embarked on the project of ascertaining her anatomy to ensure all components needed for making a baby was in place. Each of the journeys to ascertaining how her internal structure for baby-making operated proved her fit and capable to have a child yet she could not have one.

Then her husband joined in the project of testing and affirming whether he was the cause of their childlessness. Each test also showed both of them were alright. In their perpetual enigma, Charlotte became the vessel of continuous worry. Her pains and grief were long and unrelenting so that they quickly made up her physical appearance and defined her composition.

Then pressure has begun from her husband who all of a sudden ceased to be caring, loving and understanding. His transformation just came in a twinkle of an eye and in a twinkle of an eye too, Charlotte discovered pains and disappointment were her perpetual companions. Her world was not just crumbling, it was also falling on her in such a way that she could not escape.

Then in despondency, she started another journey of moving from one hospital to another as if trying to prove to the medical professionals the previous tests conducted on her were wrong.

It was in one of these journeys that she met her former colleague in secondary school whom she surprisingly discovered to be a practicing gynecologist. She had entered the general hospital that day and requested to see any doctor irrespective of specialization. Curious, the clerk directed her to Dr. Itoro Brain Etuk (former Itoro Fred). While the conversation was on-going, Itoro was the first to recognize Charlotte. She asked her familiar events and places in the past both were aware off and finally disclosed herself to Charlotte. Charlotte was enthusiastic and laughed for the first time in many months. After a prolonged moment of pleasantries, Charlotte finally required about Brain Etuk and Martina Effiong, the two friends were her best in their secondary school days.

Itoro told Charlotte how she and Brain Etuk had been married and are blessed with three children. She also told Charlotte how Martina met and fell in love with Ibanga and had been married for some pretty years now. With the moment of re-familiarization over, Charlotte confided in Itoro, not as a doctor, but as an old classmate, how slowly she is dying. She talked of the ordeals from both her family and her husband's family who have taken off her liberty by presenting and inflaming her into perpetual emotional disorder. She spoke of how her husband, through the instrumentality of his people, had moved in with another woman. Then the personal traumas she faced just to think she may after all become barren formed the phobia of her entire moments. The suffering of childlessness and even the fact that her husband would hear no story of child-adoption made her completely devastated. Then as Charlotte narrated the misfortunes of her life history to Itoro, she remembered how she once insisted on adopting a child and how her husband got her beaten to the point of death. To him, her suggestion implied her full knowledge of why she could not give birth to a child.

Amid her excruciating sufferings, she told Itoro how children mocked and ran away from her in her dream. They would boo and sometimes mob her when they had opportunity to do so. In all of these, their reason is the singular fact that she is so heartless and devilish.

'Ity, even in real life' Charlotte continued amid tears and disappointment, 'Children mock and scorn me whenever they see me. Can you imagine that on several occasions, when I attempt to carry babies of even two or three months, they would scream and end up crying the entire day?'

'Do you believe you know the cause? Itoro asked trying to connect her story with the actual problem.

'Or is there something that suggests to you that this is out of the ordinary. Look at this in another way: You have done several medical tests that confirmed you are perfectly alright. Could it be you have treated a child badly before? You know some people may get away with some deeds, but others usually don't. Check your past and find out whether any event could have any connection with the reality of things with children.'

'Ity, you know in secondary school and even in my early days in the university, I used to have some incidences with unwanted pregnancy and would flush them out each time I noticed. But I was always careful to go to the best doctors in order not to leave an after effect. So far, doctors have proven that nothing is wrong with my womb.'

'Maybe there could be something more serious than that. It could be something with the conscience and you know this is where the real problem lies. So go back home and properly search your conscience with a sole intention to connect with an important event that will point to the solution. Come to the hospital next week. I will schedule an appointment for you with our most senior gynecologist. She is a missionary expatriate and I mean she's an expert,' Itoro said.

'Thank you very much, Ity. I'm really grateful. I really pray that God have mercy on me,' Charlotte said in deep tone.

'Everything will be fine. Just do as I've told you.

'What about the rest of the Classic Four? Are you still in contact?'

'Yes, we are. It's really a shame' Charlotte said.

'What shame?' Itoro asked.

Charlotte summarily narrated the predicament Mmamma and Becky were going through.

'What about Alice?' Itoro asked.

'Alice married and was living with her husband in London. But as we speak, she is back in Nigeria because she couldn't bear the heartbreak. Her husband married another wife whom he hopes will give him children since Alice can't give him any,' Charlotte explained.

'You mean all of that happened to the famous Classic Four?' Itoro asked in great amazement.

'Can you beat that?' Charlotte said to self-paradox.

After a brief moment of silence, Charlotte said:

'Please enough of the Classic Four and its burdens of shame. So how is Martina doing? How many children does she have now? Since we left the Law School, I've not set my eyes on her. It's been pretty over eighteen years, if not nineteen now?'

'Martina is doing well with her practice. She has three children. In fact, her first son is a Reverend Father,' Itoro said.

'Wow!' Charlotte exclaimed. Then after moments of contemplation, she asked, 'how old is her first son?'

'About twenty-something. He is well above twenty', Itoro said unsuspiciously. After some moments of giving thought to her question, she asked Charlotte:

'Why the age of Martina's son?

'I just wanted to know the level of growth of her children,' Charlotte said, then added, 'I thank God for both of you. So how is Brain and the children?' Itoro assured Charlotte that everybody was fine. The conversation took a very informal perspective until both women exhausted everything on the agenda for discussion. Charlotte stood up to leave after being assured by Itoro that everything would be fine. With the final pleasantries, Itoro jammed the door behind her and headed back home.

Martina sat satisfactorily at the pool side admiring the way her beloved handsome husband was deeply involved in a swimming competition with their two children. He was lively, jovial and firmly understanding. Despite the nature of his business, he never took having a good time with his family for granted. Martina thought how greatly loving he has been since she married him about eighteen years back. She could still recount how recent the scene of their meeting looks even after eighteen years. That her husband almost worships her with unending eulogy since the day of the marriage till after having children as gown as the beautiful daughter and handsome son who were playing with him now, was something so rare an understanding among married folks. Martina could not but give great thanks to GOD for being favourable to her and her family.

As she continued in her reflection of the beautiful times she had had with her family, her phone rang. She picked it up, looked into the screen and saw it was the number of her first son, Divine. She smiled admiringly at the caller and accepted the call. From the other end came the voice of Divine who called to know how his mother was faring. Martina assured him she was fine and made enquires how he was coping with the work of GOD and trying to meet the needs of many people at the same time. After the assurance, Divine requested to speak with his Dad and other siblings. Martina handed over the phone to Ibanga, her husband who took time in speaking many teasing words into the phone; receiving compliments from the other end and giving advice as information were given him. When he finished speaking, he handed over the phone to his son and daughter who had swam close to him; listened to the conversation and smiled as it went on. When they had all taken turn in speaking with Divine, the trio went back to their unfinished competition.

Teasing and smiling endlessly at the beautiful display of bond between her husband and children, Martina was happy that Divine brought her such ecstasy and marital accuracy. Her memory lingered back to those days that it all began.

Martina returned from Abuja to Uyo after her service year. A day after she arrived home, her parents summoned her to an urgent family meeting to discuss their discovery of her pet secret. Seven years earlier, she had brought a baby boy she claimed to have given birth to an left him in the care of her maternal grandmother with a humble plea that she be humane enough to keep the identity of the baby a secret from her parents till a time the story of the child would be made public knowledge. Her grandmother who was popularly known then as Mma Makara reluctantly accepted the plea, but received the baby with all her heart. To Martina's grandmother, the coming of the baby would make up for a male child she never had. The child remained in the care of Mma Makara for four months, during which time Mr. and Mrs. Alphonsius Effiong visited her. When they asked whose baby Divine was, Mma Makara told them it was a neighbour's who had him delivered prematurely. For the next six years, Mma Makara kept the identity of the baby secret.

Then Mr. and Mrs. Alphonsius visited Mma Mbakara unexpected and still found the same child. This time he had so grown. To their astonishment, the same baby was kept with her for years without their knowledge. Surprised at her secrecy, they asked her to return the child immediately. When she refused, they threatened never to visit her again in their entire life. Pressurized, Mma Mbakara confided in them that the innocent child belonged to their daughter, Martina. Mr. and Mrs. Alphonsius Effiong were shocked beyond measure. The shock they felt left them speechless and reactionless for weeks. Then they finally decided not to confront Martina since she had just started her service year. This was to allow her concentrate and stay focused. The knowledge that Divine was their grandchild drew them to him even though they could not determine his paternity. They willingly accepted him and asked Mma Mbakara to come with him to Uyo so he can get used to his family.

So when Martina was confronted with the issue of Divine, she promised to tell them everything about Divine's birth, but she only needed to be given time. Her parents understood with her, left the matter pending and envisaged a convenient moment to understand the situation that led their well-behaved and trustworthy daughter to have a child outside wedlock.

Mr. Alphonsius Effiong arranged with a SAN friend to have Martina start off her legal practice with him. Before Martina started her two year practice in the Chamber of Udoh-Nsikak, her father bought her a Honda CR-V and had a house furnished for her.

Not long, her legal prowess could not be hidden in Udoh-Nsikak Chambers. Her boss would send her to represent him in various cases across the state. She was simply a combination of intelligence and legal wit. One day, she was to represent a client in a very dicey case. Apparently the last before she would leave Udoh-Nsikak Chamber to be on her own. In the court room, she appeared as counsel to the plaintiff who came with several of his friends to hear the proceedings of the case. Despite the intricacies of the case, Martina's presentation and cross-examination of the witnesses gave her nods of approval from every-one in the court room. Outside the courtroom, people commended her, including even her senior colleagues.

Then while Martina approached her car, she noticed a well-built young handsome man following her. As she turned backward, she discovered she was standing before a stranger who kept on smiling all the time even before he said anything. Then her client, the plaintiff for the case she just finished called out from a distance as he jogged mildly towards them. After more commendations, he introduced the smiling man to Martina as Ibanga Eton.

'Ibanga Eton is actually a businessman who imports things from various parts of the world; the plaintiff begun rendering an anecdote of Ibanga. 'Actually, he is interested in my case and came to listen to the proceedings and to determine the colour it will take. He was so thrilled when he saw a young lady like you displaying a great knowledge of legalistic power. In fact, he is contemplating monopolizing you as his personal lawyer in this generation and the one to come.'

With this, the company of three burst out in great laughter. After the round of laughter, Martina and Ibanga had time to discuss peripheral knowledge of themselves.

The plaintiff left Martina and Ibanga alone. He had finished his part of the deal. Ibanga had asked him to have him brought before Martina so he can have things easy with her. When the plaintiff contemplated turning down the request, Ibanga went all alone to Martina. When the plaintiff discovered his friend would have his way without him, he decided to come in quickly so he could share in the compliment and glory to come.

Ibanga learnt basic information he needed and employed civility to get her number. Within days Ibanga was all over Martina. He never gave her breathing space. He studied her schedules and knew her leisure. Ibanga planned his tactics diplomatically and employed most sophisticated wit to break down barriers and bring down Martina's walls, knowing too well how exposed, intelligent and sensitive she was. Martina recognized the pace with which Ibanga moved. She had no other wall apart from the resolution that any man who accepted her son, Divine, would be her husband. So, she quickly asked Ibanga to define what he wanted by pushing so hard into her world. To answer her question, Ibanga made a surprised event and a dramatic scene to tell her how he loved her and wanted to marry her as soon as possible. The story of a man being crazily in love with her was not new.

As usual, she went straight to the point. She told him she had a son and that it was a resolved issue for a man not to sleep with her before marriage. The expression on Ibanga's face was that of contentment, excitement and satisfaction. He quickly requested to meet Divine. Martina fixed date for the meeting. When the meeting between Ibanga and Divine was actualized, both of them became very fond of themselves. Something in Divine kept on attracting Ibanga and Divine almost believed Ibanga was his father. The bond between Ibanga and Divine amazed Martina and she could see a force keeping both of them together. She knew what she saw was not a charade or a false display. From the way Ibanga loved her and Divine and took both of them out for funfair almost every weekend he was less busy, she knew he would be her husband.

During Divine's birthday, Ibanga formally asked Martina to marry him. Few days later, she accepted and their wedding kicked off with all kinds of planning.

When Ibanga Eton appeared before Mr. and Mrs. Alphonsius Effiong to formally notify them of his intention to marry Martina, the first question they asked him was whether he was aware Martina had a son. He said he was. Then they asked him whether he had told his parents about his marriage and the fact that his would-be wife had already had a son for an unknown man in her final year in secondary school. Ibanga assured Mr. and Mrs Alphonsius Effiong that he told them everything that they had accepted her wholeheartedly. With the clarification of Martina's past, her parents gave consent for the marriage rites to proceed. A date was fixed and all requirements met.

Not long, Martina and Ibanga got married. Martina was fulfilled that she had kept her resolution and enforced her principle. For Ibanga Eton, he never really knew who Martina was until their honeymoon started.

The night after their wedding, the couple instinctively knew they had every right to intimately know each other. The atmosphere of the room was greatly decorated with a choice colour of pink. A mixture of miniature colour bulbs blinked and saturated the entire room with an ambience that was somewhat difficult to describe. Rose flowers were scattered on definite locations in the room and the fragrance they emitted was so inviting. Then a soft music from the home theatre player left the room an enchanting epistle at all times. Martina had just finished taking her bath. She sat down combing her hair and accosmetising herself, while waiting for Ibanga to finish in the bathroom.

When Ibanga finally emerged out of the bathroom, he saw his wife in stripped-hand and short silky pink night gown, decorated with lace buds. The gown fitted her and left her curves visible in it. The sight sent spines into Ibanga's system. He controlled himself for a while and spent time heaping decorative compliments and beautiful words of approval on her. Not satisfied, he stood silently admiring Martina without a word.

'Hey Honey,' Martina called out teasingly to him; don't look at me like that. You could at least close your so that something won't go in there because I'm going to have it on mine.'

'Honey, I never knew you are this beautiful. I'm so surprised. I thought I saw a goddess,' Ibanga said.

'Well, this goddess is here to love and cherish you all your life. Talking about surprises, I have more for you,' Martina said, smilingly at her husband. Then she said with a gesticulation, 'Come here, let's begin'.

With the invitation, Ibanga approached Martina and entered her arms. They embraced each other passionately and warmly. They spent some time caressing each other and then moved on to find each other's lips. They kissed and kissed, fondling themselves in a passion that transcended sensuality. Then they fell on the Rose-covered bed and continued the rite until they both were completely nude. Then Ibanga located his duty after he affectionately caressed Martina. His phallus broke into Martina's hymen, opening the thin layer of her vagina. She felt an excruciating pain and tried to balance off herself against the pains that forced uncomfortable sensation into all parts of her body. The bed witnessed broken stains of blood and after a while Ibanga noticed. The evidence of blood stain on the bed sheet heralded the reality of Martina's virginity.

The discovery shocked Ibanga. Never in the present age had men witnessed an exposed and sophisticated woman remaining a virgin till her marriage. Ibanga could not utter a word but fixed his gaze on Martina till he did not know what to do or how to show the immensity of his shock. The only words that proceeded out of his mouth were:

'Honey, you were a virgin?'

'You can answer that. Or are you not convinced?' Martina said rhetorically.

Then the thought about Divine, and the enigma surrounding the whole event. How can his wife, a virgin who had known no man before gave birth to Divine.

'So what about Divine, Honey?' Ibanga asked.

'I knew for certain you will ask this question. Divine is not my biological son. I suffered four heartbreaks because of him. I knew none of those men were mine. I made a resolution that a man who will accept Divine as his son will be my husband. GOD answered my prayer when you came my way; Martina explained.

'How did Divine come?' Ibanga asked.

'Well, that is a story I will not want to repeat. I will say it just once in the midst of people concerned', Martina said.

'How do you mean?' Ibanga asked.

'For the past eight years, I've kept the secret surrounding Divine's birth away from everyone. My parents, grandmother and friends who helped me raise Divine do not know neither do they have a glimpse of the story surrounding Divine's birth. I want everybody present so I can tell the story.'

'Okay. But in addition to that, I will show this to your parents, my parents and everyone that I married you a virgin. Like tradition demands, I will honour your father for bringing you up in great honour. As for you Honey, you are the world to me. What you did is the most important gift I've received and will ever receive. In this twenty-first century, I married an intelligent, beautiful and sophisticated woman like you a virgin? It's not found anywhere in the world and so rare!' Ibanga enthused.

The next day, Ibanga summoned all the elders of his family, his parents; Martina's Parents, their extended family members, his friends, Martina's friends and other people immediately important to the event to an urgent meeting in Mr. and Mrs. Alphonsius Effiong's compound. Martina personally sent for her grandmother, Mma Mbakara and brought her in her car to the meeting. Just before the meeting started, Ibanga had sent for all items recognized by tradition as mark to honour his wife's family in moments of such discovery.

The invitee's attended the meeting in great curiosity. Everyone was eager to know what the promptness of such a meeting heralded, but could not as they could neither guess nor foretell the sudden event that warranted the gathering. When the house was full with elders from both Ibanga and Martina's families, Ibanga brought all items he had bought to the middle of the meeting. The curiosity of those present increased and they only struggled to patiently wait for Ibanga to address them. Then finally, Ibanga stepped out to the floor, greeted the elders and started speaking in relevant proverbs. The men nodded in agreement and bade him go straight to the point.

After series of more comments, Ibanga announced to the gathering that he married Martina a virgin. Astonishment and reflection of impossibility resurrected on the faces of the elders. Then Ibanga produced the bedspread of proof and showed it to the entire gathering. They all scrutinized it and recognized it was so. Then almost at the same time, the men asked Ibanga the same question he asked Martina. They all wanted to know how a virgin could give birth to a son like Divine. To clarify the curiosity of everyone gathered, Ibanga made a gesture to Martina who stepped forward and told everyone the full story of what she knew about Divine's birth. After the story, Martina's dignity and integrity increased in the eyes of everyone. She had commendations upon commendations and all kinds of approval. Her parents were even more proud of her and declared that she was the major source of their honour. Then her husband, Ibanga consciously respected and loved her for eighteen years of marriage. In fact, after eighteen years of marriage, it looks like Ibanga continuously fell in love with her over and over again.

CHAPTER THREE

Mmamma Teddy Anieboanam had stopped going to work. Her grief did not allow her stay in the midst of people. She had locked herself away from her mother and mother-in-law for days and continued to weep day-in and day-out. She did not reconcile why life treated her so harshly and yet was not done punishing her. In the midst of her grief, she heard another round of knock. She knew who the knockers were. They were her mother and mother-in-law. The two women had been running from one point to another just to search out a lasting solution to her childlessness. This time, they knocked and knocked without relenting until she had an impulse to open up the door to them.

When they came in, they consoled her and also reprimanded her for tormenting herself to the point of living in sorrow and staying away from her job. After sometime of maternal consolation, Mmamma relaxed for a while before the two women announced their findings.

'What findings,' Mmamma asked curiously.

'After the man of God finished praying for you on our behalf, he said the LORD revealed that your calamity persists because you had wronged the innocent in the past,' Mmamma's mother-in-law said

'What innocent?' Mmamma exclaimed in shock.

Charlotte had called her two days earlier to announce how she had gone to see a pastor to have headway for her predicament, only to be told she had conspired against the innocent. The information kept on ringing over her conscience. She searched and searched herself until she seemed to have stumbled over the actual problem. She could remember how sexually loose she, and her three other friends were in their days in secondary school. She did not believe that her conscience was murdered to the point of committing such a terrible abomination she had just reminisced. Her guilt continuously gnawed them and now she could no longer blame GOD for what was happening to them, but herself. It was clear she deserved to suffer this agony for her inhumanity.

The next morning, Mmamma decided to pack out of the house, she did not want Teddy to continue to suffer and pay unjustly for her own sin. After packing her things, she left a note for Teddy. As she secretly left the house, tears flowed down her cheeks uncontrollably. Then after admiring a small portrait of Teddy, she pocketed it and left the house quietly without the notice of anyone. She boarded taxi to Charlotte's place to see how to sort out their unfortunate nemeses.

Charlotte came forward to open the door immediately she heard the bell ring. Surprised to see Mmamma, she hugged her dearly and ushered her into the house. What Mmamma saw shocked her the more. There was Becky wrapped in bandage and groaning in pains. Mmamma embraced Becky and enquired what happened. As she opened her mouth to narrate the unfortunate situation, she broke down in tears. Charlotte took up the story and explained how Kokoette had gotten a woman pregnant and brought her to their matrimonial home. When Becky tried to find out why the woman was in the house, Kokoette not only told her the lady was pregnant with his baby, but also spent time in beating her up.

'Why is this befalling four of us, Charlotte?' Mmamma lamented. 'Why must we be suffering the consequences of our past in this degree?'

'Consequences of our past?' Both Becky and Charlotte exclaimed rhetorically at the same time.

'How?' Becky asked. After a moment of brief thought, she added, 'wait a minute! I hope it's not what I think?'

In reply, Charlotte and Mmamma nodded in affirmation.

'So what do we do now?' Becky asked worried.

'The Pastor who revealed it to me said I need to find the innocent I wronged and beg for forgiveness, otherwise I will die barren, and you know, this applies to four of us,' Charlotte said.

'God forbid!' Becky and Mmamma exclaimed simultaneously.

With that, Mmamma burst out in great weeping. As she wept, Charlotte phone rang. It was Alice! She had called Charlotte to announce her coming. Not long, she arrived. Immediately she was inside the sitting room, she crashed on the floor and wept terribly. Mmamma held her peace and joined the other two to watch Alice display such a terrible mood. However, they consoled her and got her calm. When she held her peace, the other three women encouraged her to speak.

Then she told them how in a bid to ascertain the root of her problem, her mother took her to a Prophet who narrated the story of her life to her. He had told her how she and her three friends committed an abomination when they were still young. The result of that abomination is their childlessness. The only way they all can escape is praying to God for forgiveness and also seeking the forgiveness of the wronged. With that Alice fell on the floor weeping and lamenting.

'I've suffered almost twenty years of childlessness. The insults and humiliations I passed through in London are better imagined than told. Imagine how I thought I was enjoying, but never knew in reality I was laying a sorrowful and disgusting foundation for my future! How else can I explain this? How can I explain that few years of thrills and supposed enjoyment could cause me a long time of shame, mockery and humiliation… GOD, help me! GOD, help me!' Alice screamed and sobbed in great pains.

Charlotte, Mmamma and Becky immediately sat together discussing what to do in order to resolve and walk out of their curse. Not long, Alice joined them. With the four of them present, they talked how they may collectedly seek the face of GOD for forgiveness, and then go in search for the innocent one they conspired against and wronged. How time flies. The four women who once knew themselves as 'The Classic Four' in their teenage years could not but sit and reflect on the vanities of unproductive actions people take as priorities only to be in bondage and perpetual agony for the rest of their lives.

Ibanga and Martina agreed it was necessary to intimate Divine of the circumstance of his birth. He was already twenty-five years of age and needed to understand the reality of his root. However, they both agreed he was their son and nothing changed to this regard. After due consideration and approval, both parents summoned Divine to a family meeting later in the evening. Before he finally came to see them, he attended the evening mass. At home, Ibanga and Martina exchanged pleasantries with Divine, showed him to a sumptuous dinner and allowed him to take a brief rest.

Then the big hour came. Ibanga teasingly made the atmosphere less tense before telling Divine he needed to know a little secret they both had kept away from him. He told Divine both of them never wanted him to hear it from the mouth of a stranger, hence they both considered it appropriate to let him into it. Ibanga further stated that Divine was grown and needed to learn how to handle issues like a man. He continued his preparatory exhortation amid the puzzle reflected on the face of the young man. When he had stabilized the atmosphere, Ibanga nodded to Martina to take over the scene and make the narration as it happened. Martina started:

'My son, this secret doesn't and will not change anything we are to you. Just as your father has said, the secret is just for information,' she paused. Then she resumed in a more dramatic manner. 'My son, we are not your biological parent!'

The information stunned Divine who instinctively had the following words emerged out of his mouth:

'I beg your pardon, Mum. What sort of joke is that?'

Martina calmed her son down, who was covered up by emotions of disappointment. Despite the love and pity she felt for him at such a sensitive moment, she believed it was only necessary and appropriate to make him know the truth.

'Beloved, it's not a joke. You know you're my love. So keep away this hard feeling and listen to me.'

Divine tried hard to suppress the rage. Having surmounted his first shock, he sat quietly and listened to his mother. Martina looked at Ibanga who gave an approval to continue. She cleared her throat and started the story.

'It happened twenty-five years ago. I was in my final year in High School and also preparing for our certificate examination. We were having our extension classes as it's the tradition for final year students. We were in a class waiting for the teacher to come, when all of a sudden I became so pressed. I left the class for convenience. Once I was out of the class, I wandered instinctively beyond the place of convenience and enjoyed myself walking towards a direction I never would want to go normally. Just by the bush which was completely secluded and bereft of all students and passers-by, I stood to urinate. But just then I heard voices which came to me like people having slight argument. I quickly suspended my system and walked towards the direction where the voices were coming from.

'To my greatest surprise, I saw the four girls who were my classmates and whose group was popularly called the Classic Four. They were Mmamma, Becky or Rebecca, Charlotte and Alice. While peeping and eavesdropping on their conversations I heard the following: "Kill him or what do you intend to do? Becky instructed.

"I can imagine she wants to show the School Authority or her parents she has a child in High School,' Charlotte scolded and mocked at the same time.

Just then, I discovered a handsome baby soaked in womb blood. He had just been given birth to. As the three girls were pressurizing the owner of the baby, she went closer to the crying child, lifted her foot and tried to smash him to death, but could not. Then she paused a while and looked at him in pity.

'But immediately she ceased from smashing him,' Alice screamed: Mma, kill this baby or I'm out of here; then you will face the music all alone!'

Mmamma loved her baby and didn't want to kill him, but she was afraid of being rejected by her friends. Just then, she made another attempt to smash him, when I screamed at her to stop such a bastardly act. The four of them froze and turned to my direction in great shock. Then I said to them, "Why are you so wicked and heartless? Mmamma, so you want to kill this innocent child just because your 'Classic Four' friends say you should do so? Where is your conscience? Why would you carry this child for that long, only for you to kill him after delivery? You go ahead and kill him and see if you will not explain to the school Authority.'

Then the rest of the three girls turned to attack me. They mockingly called me 'Good Samaritan.' Just then, Mmamma made another round of attempt to smash the baby to death, but I interrupted her. After threatening them and showing them the possibility of executing my threats, they gave up the idea of murdering the baby and sought an alternative. After many suggestions, the four of them agreed to take the baby to the chaplain's wife. But they decided that he be put into a carton and dumped at the ravine behind the chaplain's house and there was a probability for the chaplain's wife or anyone else to see him and pick up.

"What happens if the Chaplain's wife doesn't go there today?" I had asked them.

"Then he dies. That way, we will have no hand in his death!" Becky had declared nonchalantly.

So the four of them wrapped the baby in carton and took him to the ravine. While they were heading there, I secretly followed them to find out the exact spot they would leave the baby. Satisfied they never killed him as planned, I left. At night, I returned alone to find out whether the Chaplain's wife had picked the baby. When I returned, I saw the innocent child in the dark crying and very hungry. So I returned to the dormitory, took money and went back to the ravine. I picked him up and took him to my maternal grandmother who was popularly called Mma mbakara and left him in her care. Before I left the following morning, I told her the child's name was Divine. After assuring me she would take good care of him until I was ready to have him stay with me, I left. But I was always so careful that my baby was well fed, catered for and sent to school. That was twenty-five years ago! But as he grew up, I met my beloved husband who also joined in fathering him; she paused a while and looked at Divine who was awestruck at the story.

'You see, my son, that little child of mine turned out to be this tall, handsome, intelligent young man gazing lovingly at me,' Martina said.

Tears ran down the eyes of Divine. He moved close to Martina and engaged her in long embrace. Then after disengaging himself from her, he hugged Ibanga before saying few words of gratitude and his passionate love for his parents. Then Divine remembered how a woman came for a confession and gave similar story. To him, he felt the woman had a conviction with his birth. He logically wandered if the woman's story has any relativity to his parent's revelation. When he could not reach a proper conclusion, he decided to see the unfolding of things as the days approached. Whatever colour the event would turn out to wear, time was the only factor that could decide. The three of them spent more time discussing other weighty matters.

Mmamma, Charlotte, Becky and Alice decided to visit their past. The four women finally bowed to the power of nemesis. They collectively agreed to acknowledge that day, ignored part of their past they erroneously adjudged powerless and silent, but unbelievably turned out to be the major determiner of their womanhood and marital fate. So the four women went back to the ravine they had dumped Divine twenty-five years early. At the exact spot the baby was dumped in moments their teenage spirit was the only motivating force, Mmamma broke down and wept profusely. The spot seemed to bring back that part of her past she thought she had escaped from. So touched that they had been major bad influence on her, the three friends could not hold their peace but joined her in crying. When they had nearly exhausted their pains, they collectively consoled Mmamma.

Then Alice suggested they find out whether the Chaplain's wife took the baby in as they intended as 'Option B'. Charlotte opposed the idea and explained how preposterous it sounded and appeared. Becky then exclaimed 'what sort of a dump thought is that in the first place. I guess you will just walk into somebody's house and ask: "Madam, did you take a baby at the ravine some twenty-five years ago?"

'There is always a way to take in finding things out; so we have to think,' Alice said in explication.

'Alice is right. Please, let us think of something,' Mmamma said in desperate anxiety.

With that, the four women headed to the direction leading to the Chaplain's house. In front of the house, they met a parishioner who told them the Chaplain was posted out about twelve years earlier to another location and finally retired two years after. The news blew off the four women and they reluctantly turned back and went back home in the midst of pricking consciences.

Immediately the four women stepped into Charlotte's compound, they were all so shocked to see Teddy walking anxiously to and fro in worried strides. Mmamma greeted him warmly and politely requested to know how he got to know she was at Charlotte's place since the note she left him was not exact with her whereabouts. Teddy simply replied that it was obvious she could be in no one else's place than Charlotte's.

'How serious was the secret that made you to pack out of the house without my knowledge?' Teddy begun in an angry voice he forced under control. 'Wasn't it necessary for you to intimate me with the secret no matter how worst it sounds and——'

'Ted please!' Mmamma interrupted him in a pleading voice that was so devastated. 'I guess you have a right to know but....' With that, she broke down crying terribly until her friends came out to plead with Teddy to drop off the matter since it was too weighty for Mmamma at the moment. An hour and some minutes, Mmamma narrated the entire episode to Teddy and persuaded him to pick a new wife who would give him a child. But before making her genuine suggestion, she spent time begging Teddy for forgiveness for wasting away his beautiful time he would have enjoyed as a supermodel father his children would have been proud of. But Teddy waved away

Mmamma suggestions and her guilt of parental obstacle by declaring how he would stand by her no matter the storm. He immediately proffered relative suggestions to the resolution of the situation and even offered to go with his wife to trace out the Chaplain at his new point of duty before he retired.

The following day, the four women set out to trace the Chaplain with the address they received from the parishioner. After a tedious investigation and good time spent in enquiries, they finally appeared before the Chaplain. The old man could not recognize who his august guests were. All the same, he employed courtesy to ensure the intention of the meeting was not distorted. The four ladies were unnecessarily nice to the Chaplain who was careful not to rush of the edge to misjudge matters. Finally, the women explained they had taken the school certificate exams sometime in 1983 and the Chaplain's wife so much found them agreeable to her good judgment. In fact, they told the man how sorry they were not to visit all those years even after they heard the old man's wife had given birth to a handsome baby boy almost the year they left school. Then they imagined how grown the boy must have been into a handsome looking young man, hence they decided to pay the Chaplain's wife the visit they would have paid her twenty-five years earlier.

The Chaplain patiently listened to the four women and allowed them exhaust their hilarious acclamations before speaking up. The old man's face was bereft of all forms of expression. He was neither sad nor happy; hence his face was so straight, formal and a little bit mixed with courtesy. He calmly corrected the women. He told them his wife never gave birth to a son until ten years earlier. Second, he told them his wife gave birth to a female child, not a male and she is the only child they have. Then he took their attention to the image of the girl which hung on the opposite wall of the sitting room. To add a little detail to the impossibility of their mission, he told them the girl and her mother was in the United States of America for a long vacation. After counteracting their assertions, the Chaplain apologized to the women for grossly being misinformed and concluded by judging their visit a necessary voluntary act of maturity. Then the four women handed him an envelope of money to seal off the deal of their courtesy visit.

As they stepped out of the house, they found the caretaker and engaged him in clarification enquiries. The women wanted to know how many children the Chaplain had and whether he had any adopted child. The caretaker unknowingly confirmed everything the old man had told them some minutes before. Satisfied that the Chaplain never had the child they were looking for, the women drove off.

When they arrived home, the four women discovered how difficult and unpredictable their situation was metamorphosing into. Nothing crossed their minds except to go back in fasting and asking GOD to have mercy on them. As the process continued and the four women cried desperately for help, then Charlotte jumped up suddenly in great exclamation:

'I've got it! I've got it.'

The other three women suddenly stopped praying to watch Charlotte. She continued to exclaim until the three held her and requested she shared what it was that got her so excited. She paused for a while, gazed at her three friends before smiling mystically.

'The boy we are searching for is probably the same boy Martina claims to be her first son,' Charlotte explained.

'How? What do you mean?' Mmamma asked in increased interest.

'Probably? We need certainty, not probability,' Alice said slightly angry.

'Go ahead, tell us why you think so,' Becky said.

'You three remember that Martina was the person who prevented us from killing that innocent child?' Charlotte asked.

The three women sat reminiscing before admitting slowly and irregularly depending on the speed of their individual memory.

'I remember!' Mmama exclaimed. 'Martina Alphonsius Effiong was the angel who spared the boy's life when we had concluded plans to smash him to death. Why did I not remember that before now?'

'So what are you saying Charly? Are you saying Martina has the boy we are looking for?' Becky said in curiosity.

'I'm sure. You bet that,' Charlotte said.

'Why are you that sure?' Alice asked.

'Yes, why are you that sure?' Becky concurred.

'Martina is only married for eighteen years now, but she already has a son who is up to twenty-five years. How is that possible? You and I know Martina was not popular with men even an inch. We could conclude she hated men and even up to the point I met her at the Law School, she still never contemplated having any relationship with any man. So how could she have had an opportunity to mother a twenty-five year old son? Even the other time, I heard Itoro Brian Etuk saying Martina made her parents proud for being herself till marriage. I don't know what Itoro meant by that, but I personally take it to mean Martina may have married a virgin. If this is true, only one woman gave birth to a son on earth while still was a virgin. I'm not sure any ordinary mortal will do so again,' Charlotte said.

'Charlotte has a point there,' Becky said. 'I can now vividly remember that it was Martina who was aware we would leave the child at the ravine spot. Since we just need to ask the child to forgive and bless us, let's plan how to break into Martina and subsequently have access to the now grown up son:

'We have to be sure the young man in question is the same I gave birth to some twenty-five years, else we may be trading on dangerous ground,' Mmamma said.

'So what do we do now?' Alice said a little impatient.

'I think I have an idea,' Charlotte said. 'I will ascertain the true state of the matter by talking to Itoro tomorrow morning in her office. In fact, her body language will confirm my conviction. I don't think it's possible for Itoro not to know the maternity of the child.'

'Good. That sounds better,' Alice and Becky exclaimed simultaneously.

Charlotte did as planned the following day.

Immediately the pleasantries were over with Itoro, Charlotte brought up the issue. At first, Itoro attacked Charlotte about the absurdity of even thinking Divine was not Martina's son. Then Charlotte changed her composure by trying to get Itoro sympathetic to her predicament and that of her friends. Itoro watched her silently for a while in pity before concluding and advising Charlotte sees Martina and gets a fair hearing since she had no knowledge of what she was talking about. Satisfied at Itoro's expression, Charlotte left the office and went straight to her friends to render account of her progress report.

The four women became optimistic and took steps to visit Martina on a target hour Charlotte planned would not coincide with her court case that same day. Just as Charlotte had rightly thought, the four women met Martina when she was already at leisure. After moment of self-explanation, recognition and acknowledgement, Martina offered them an exquisite settee in her office and ordered drinks for them. Martina did not or refused to suspect the intention of the women's visit. All along, she kept on teasing and commending them for staying together as the 'Classic Four' for that number of years. Mmamma, Becky, Alice and Charlotte all took turns in heaping encomiums on her for her legal prowess that kept the city on genuine gossip. Martina acknowledged the compliments and told them how greatly her husband, Ibanga supported and contributed to her legal success.

'Charlotte, I didn't see you at the last legal council meeting. Are you alright with your practice? In fact, recently your appearances in court have been so scarce or irregular. Do you have any personal challenge with your private practice? Martina asked Charlotte in genuine concern.

'Well Martina, you are right. Probably that is why I'm here with my friends. I really hope you can help me recover my sanity so I can be focused with legal practice,' Charlotte said.

'Well, anything within my power I can do. It takes nothing to help a friend,' Martina said.

With that, Charlotte beckoned Mmamma to present the matter.

'Tina, we shouldn't disturb you with facts that seemed almost completely dead in the past. We can't help but come to you so we may reconcile with our past and live like any other normal being on earth. Please pardon us for bringing up this burden now,' Mmamma said.

'What is it? Go ahead. Say it, I'm all ears' Martina encouraged the uncourageous Mmamma.

'We are here in respect of the baby,' Mmamma said, almost struggling to be audible.

'What baby?' Martina asked in shock and realizing for the first time, the complete presence of all the party involved.

'The same baby you saw me give birth to during our extension classes,' Mmamma said in subdued mood

'What about the baby?' Martina asked formally. She knew a day like this would come. So she remained confident and undisturbed.

'We found out that the Chaplain's wife did not take the baby as planned and you were the only person directly involved in the secret,' Mmamma said, trying hard to prevent her tears.

'So indirectly I took the baby?' Martina asked with full gaze on Mmamma.

Mm... I mean...' I mean...Mmamma stammered, trying hard to find words of courtesy.

'Well, the baby must have been dead or eaten up by some animals just as you intended,' Martina said.

'So who's Father Divine?' Charlotte cut in impatiently and angrily.

'What nonsense! Martina exclaimed. 'Father Divine is my son. I think I have a right to my privacy.'

'How is it possible to be married for only eighteen years and have a son of twenty-five years?'

'With due respect lady!' Martina exclaimed. 'You have no right to invade my privacy in such a provocating manner!'

The other three turned to Charlotte in great attack. They scolded and reprimanded her for trying to close a door of solution to their predicament. When they had accomplished their session, they turned to Martina and placated her. When she was assuaged, she opened up to them:

'Well, Father Divine is the same baby four of you conspired to kill twenty-five years ago by induced abortion and abandonment. As you all know, he is now my son and nothing can change that. If this is all you wanted to know, you can be sure you have it right. But be rest assured that no one can claim my son. It will neither happen in my life time nor in my death.' She paused for a while before saying: Ladies or whatever you call yourselves, you can now leave my office. I'm done with you!'

As Martina ordered the women out of her office, she barred the door behind them.

On their way home, Mmamma, Becky and Alice blamed Charlotte for blowing up their plan and by extension cutting off what they would have achieved. Charlotte defended herself by threatening to take the case to court, but the other three women reminded her about the criminality of child abandonment and even attempted murder. They all returned to Charlotte's house to re-strategize steps to penetrate Martina and convince her of making Divine see them. This obviously was a strenuous process but they also knew how vital it was if their marital identity was to be reversed.

CHAPTER FOUR

Martina returned home very angry. She was so determined to fight anyone who came laying claim on her son. Her husband, Ibanga was sitting in the parlour cuddling a magazine which specialized in showing hidden uniqueness of most countries of the world when she walked into the house, greeted him and went straight to the room. Ibanga knew something was certainly wrong. So he tried to get her to talk about it, but when she declined, he gave it up.

At bedtime, Martina's mood had not completely improved. So Ibanga gently suggested series of possible events in order to get his wife talk about the seeming heavy burden that systematically ate her up. Finally, Martina told Ibanga that the self-styled 'Classic Four' came to her office to lay claims to Divine. Ibanga trivialized the matter by assuring Martina not to lose sleep over insignificant matters since both of them would fight whoever tries to lay claim on Divine.

Two days later, two of the Classic Four, Mmamma and Alice returned to Martina's office to beg her for an audience with Divine so they could be released from the silent curse that so much determined to wipe the four of them out of life without conception. Martina bluntly told them she would not subject her son into a bitter experience by allowing a dirty past get up to an enjoyable present. With that, Mmamma fell on her knees as she pleaded.

'Please Tina, help us out. I'm a woman in great predicament and my soul has been saddened for a long time. My friends and I have been suffering from this wickedness for a long time. Tina, look at me and be merciful. I've suffered six miscarriages at the seventh month in twenty years of marriage. I am even meant to die, but GOD just spared my life up to this point. We just want to see him and beg for forgiveness so our soul can be released from this persisting torment. I can't struggle over him with you. I'm not worthy to have him. I left him to die in the cold and would even have killed him if not for your timely intervention. I have absolutely no right to call him my son. All I seek is his forgiveness. At least, I could tell him how sorry I am. We just want GOD to forgive us,' Mmamma said, crying profusely and regrettably.

Seeing how unmoved Martina stood staring at Mmamma, Alice joined her friend. She fell on her knees and continued begging Martina.

'Please Martina, forgive us and grant Mma audience with the boy. All of us are suffering from one thing or the other because of this. Tina, I'm barren and gynecologists in the whole of London could not find out what is wrong with me. As I speak, my husband has taken another wife all because I cannot give him a child. Please have mercy, Tina,' Alice said, sobbing.

The continued sobbing and lamentations of the women penetrated the depth of Martina, but she all the same tried not to be influenced. After much contemplations, Martina declared how she could not take the place of GOD in showing anyone mercy, hence denied the women access to Divine. But they continued a parade of begging for mercy until Martina discovered she may not escape the invasion of the weeping women and would have to miss most of her important schedules.

'Okay, okay, okay,' Martina said in fast voice as she begun in giving her consent. 'Please put yourselves together. You know how uneasy this process would be. In as much as I'm so much concerned about your plight, I cannot take an independent decision. I have to seek my husband's consent. If he accepts, well, I'll grant you access to Divine. But if he doesn't I can do nothing. I just hope I can help, but I promise nothing,' Martina told them.

Hours metamorphosed into days and days into weeks, the four women never heard from Martina. Moreso, it surprisingly became so uneasy to get her. All efforts to get to her became so frustrating until Mmamma isolated herself and would eat nothing until she be brought before her son. Her friends called her husband who came immediately and persuaded her to open the door. Still, she refused to eat, but locked herself away from the eyes of everyone. Teddy and her three friends tried all they could to ameliorate her self-inflicted predicament.

Day after day, Mmamma continued to depreciate until her three friends joined her husband and attempted to break down the door, but she threatened to commit suicide if the dared tamper with the door. Mmamma was sore stern. She told them that she wanted to die by any means and the only thing that will stop her death was an audience with Fr. Divine. Teddy felt great pains hung all over his wife's voice, yet he could do nothing to solvent her agonies. Afraid that Mmamma might eventually commit suicide, Teddy and Alice went back to Martina to plead if at least she could grant her audience with Divine. Teddy was on his knees begging for the life of his wife, almost in tears. At this point, Martina and Ibanga could not watch such emotional outburst and decided to grant Mmamma audience with Divine. Immediately, Ibanga and Martina summoned Divine to the house for an urgent meeting. Then Martina, Teddy and Alice went back to get Mmamma and others.

With the breaking news, Mmamma suddenly regained strength and flaunted the door open. In few minutes, they set out to Ibanga and Martina's family home. Ibanga was waiting for the arrival of Divine, as Martina, Mmamma, Teddy and the rest of the Classic Four arrived. Teddy spoke to Ibanga and Martina about their humane character and unusual kindness. He thanked them for their lavish display of love and most importantly, for their reconsideration to grant his wife audience to the young man. Ibanga and Martina acknowledged Teddy's gratitude and thoughtfulness and assured Mmamma and her friends that everything would be alright. With this, Alice and Becky fell on their knees and thanked Ibanga and Martina for their magnanimity and thanking God for solving the lurking peril that would have lasted eternally.

At this point, Divine entered the house and found a semi-crowd. At first, he was astonished for unplanned, unannounced and uninformed meeting, but immediately scanned through the faces present that were so unfamiliar. Ibanga and Martina noticed how stunned he was entering the somehow crowded sitting room, Ibanga went to him across the room where he stood and began to placate him. He placed his hand across Divine's shoulder and tried to calm him down, assuring him that there was nothing so serious. When everyone duly sat down, Ibanga intimated Fr. Divine the reason for the emergency meeting.

'Dad, I don't think this whole thing is proper right now,' Divine begun his complaint. 'This woman thinks she can spring up from nowhere like mushroom to claim what she is not. This is impossible! I had no idea that your distress call was all about this. Of course, I wouldn't have bothered coming.'

'Son, calm down. Please just calm down and know that everything will be fine. I don't know how you feel, but I do know you are not happy. Trust me, this will be over. You have to face this once and for all. It changes nothing we are to you, whether now or after now,' Ibanga assured Divine.

With that, Divine proceeded to embrace Martina.

'Honey, you are here!' Martina greeted her son.

'Mum, so you are a part of this,' Divine told Martina calmly.

'Son, it's not what you think. Just believe me. This is a matter of life and death. You just have to hear her out,' Martina assured Divine. Then turning to Mmamma, she made gesture to her to start talking to Divine.

Mmamma went straight to Fr. Divine, and stood in front of him before explaining summarily why she ignorantly abandoned him. After her statement of remorse and assertion of how unworthy she was to have Divine as her son, she went on her knees in tears.

'Father,' Mmamma addressed Divine as she begun, 'please in the name of GOD forgive me! I am truly sorry for all that happened. I'm not asking for a chance to be your mother because I stand truly unjustified.'

Turning to Charlotte, Becky and Alice, Mmamma made a gesture to them. They joined her, kneeling in front of Divine. With one voice, they all began to beg Divine to forgive them.

'My friends and I have suffered deeply and unquantifiably because of our teenage foolishness. Please forgive me. Just find a place in your heart to forgive us,' Mmamma said, weeping profusely.

As she cried, her three friends continued begging for his forgiveness. Divine remained silent for awhile, watching the seeming unusual spectacle in great amazement, rather than in interest. Then Mmamma held the hem of Divine's Cassock for a long time. Her friends joined her in the rite until Divine cleared his throat in sympathy.

'I forgive you and all of your friends in Jesus name,' Divine declared to Mmamma and her three friends. 'I pray that the Almighty GOD bless you from now and grant you your deepest desire in the Name of GOD the Father, the Son and the Holy Spirit'. Demonstrating the sign of the Cross. 'Amen!' the four women and everyone in the house echoed in enthusiasm.

Divine helped Mmamma up and her three friends. When they all stood on their feet, Divine embraced his biological mother and kissed her forehead. Then he took turn in embracing Charlotte, Alice and Becky. This done, he went to Martina and engaged her in a prolonged embrace until everyone could see the passion that tied both mother and son together. Leaving Martina, he took almost the same time in embracing Ibanga. Just then, Divine turned to see Mmamma gazing firmly at Ibanga and Ibanga gazing fixedly at her the same time. Every one's eyes, including Martina's were focused on both of them. As the thorough gaze continued, streams of recollections flooded into the memory of Ibanga.

Ibanga and Mmamma had sexual relationship some twenty-six years earlier: The outcome of the affair resulted into pregnancy. Informed of Mmamma's pregnancy, Ibanga instructed Mmamma to keep the baby, but she objected and sought to terminate it. In her adamancy, she requested Ibanga to give her money for abortion. He told her how he never had money for such a risky adventure, which may turn out deadly for Mmamma. Besides, he wanted to marry Mmamma and would inform his parents to ameliorate or eliminate all possible controversy concerning her pregnancy. But Mmamma exploded.

'IB, I hate you! GOD! You are so selfish. You want to thwart my future. Haa! Let me clearly announce to you that it won't work! For crying out loud! You have graduated and about leaving for your NYSC, but you want me to drop out of high school, stay at home and nurse your pregnancy. You had better think rightly. Whether you bring me the money or not, I can never keep this pregnancy. Period!'

With that, she walked out of Ibanga. Few days after, Ibanga came to announce to Mmamma he would be leaving for the NYSC camp.

'Why are you telling me? Have you come with the money? Or do you want me to come with you to camp? Mmamma said sarcastically.

'No. But why are you sounding this way? Ibanga said.

'No? You have not come with the money,' She repeated her question.

'No!' Ibanga replied.

'Then you have no business being here. You had better leave now!' Mmamma ordered him.

'Mma, you have less than three months to stay in school.

Besides, you are almost five months gone with the pregnancy and yet it isn't obvious. Even if it were to be, my parents can take care of everything. You will write your exams and make it to the university without having the delivery of the baby distract you. After the delivery of the baby, my mother will take care of the baby...'

'Shut up your mouth, IB,' Mmamma interrupted Ibanga.'Do you think it's a child's play to mother a baby. Well, as you see, I'm not ready to become a mother. Not just yet. You may now take your leave. Excuse me.'

With that, she walked away. Ibanga never saw her again till he returned from NYSC a year later. When he enquired after the baby who was already five months in the womb before he left, Mmamma bluntly told him she did abort the pregnancy immediately he left. Shocked, Ibanga told her how heartless she was and severed the relationship.

'Does it look like I care? Let me tell you how long I ended this mess of a relationship when I realized how selfish you were. Please leave before my parents come and meet you here!' Mmamma said impertinently.

Trying to control his anger, Ibanga remained silent and walked away.

'Good riddance to bad rubbish!' Mmamma exclaimed after him.

Ibanga turned again and looked at her pitifully in anger before finally increasing his pace.

After telling everyone present his unfortunate encounter with Mmamma many years back, Ibanga sat down holding his head regrettably. Then he heard the slow calm and powerful voice of Mmamma declaring in great confidence:

'Reverend Father Divine is truly your son, Mister Ibanga Eton.' He is the same child I spent all the months trying to abort, but could not. I gave birth to him after you left for NYSC'.

Then turning to Divine, Mmamma announced to him:

'Ibanga is truly your biological father. You are his direct blood!'

The relation startled everyone. However, Mmamma could not withstand the shock of the entire incident. So she fainted and was quickly rushed to Itoro's hospital. Apart from the slight set-back of Mmamma's case, the day was a beautiful one for Ibanga, Martina and Divine. They finally agreed to have a get-together party to celebrate their victory despite those hard and trying moments.

At the hospital, Teddy, Charlotte, Becky and Alice waited patiently at the reception for the doctor to determine what was wrong with Mmamma and the possible solution. After a relatively long period, they saw Mmamma being taken to emergency unit of the hospital. There the doctor stayed as if she would not return. After a while, the doctor approached the small gathering and assured them of Mmamma's fitness. Then Teddy was taken aside and congratulated. In curiosity, he asked what he is being congratulated for.

'Your wife is pregnant! Itoro declared.

'Pregnant? Teddy froze in shock and stood expressionless.

The other women overheard the announcement and were engulfed in great surprise. The unfolding episode sounded more like a fairy tale than reality.

'You said my wife is pre.….? In fact, if this is a joke, we can suspend it for now, because I'm only interested in my wife's health,' Teddy said in an afterthought reaction.

'Mister Teddy, I'm too professional to be joking about sensitive issues. In fact, your wife is two months pregnant!' Itoro said, trying to establish Teddy's senses with reality.

With that, he jumped unconsciously embraced Itoro for some seconds before jumping towards the direction of the women. His reaction aroused the spontaneous reactions of the women who screamed for joy and did short dance steps. Just then, Ibanga and Martina joined the group and also heard the good news. The atmosphere of jubilation quickly robbed off on them. Ibanga embraced Teddy whose tears of joy already trickled in streams down his cheeks. Martina took turn in congratulating Teddy. After a moment, the doctor approved their entrance to see Mmamma. The jubilation continued until two days later when she was discharged.

Mmamma returned in full health to their home, while Alice and Becky continued to stay with Charlotte. Then Becky began to be feverish. At first she thought it was Malaria and applied self-medication as its common among Nigerians. But instead, the situation grew worse until Charlotte persuaded her to go see a doctor. She continued to object till Charlotte stood on her neck and forced her to go the hospital through unrestrained persuasions. She obliged and they both left.

Less than two hours after they returned from the hospital, a knock was heard at the door. Charlotte went to attend to the guest only for her to see Kokoette Attah, Becky's husband. She ignored him and made to return into the house without granting him access. He pleaded and humbly addressed Charlotte who could not resist his civility. After reprimanding him for beating and disgracing his wife out of the house, she reluctantly went inside to get Becky. Becky emerged, not strong and struggling to maintain her self-balance. Immediately she saw him, her countenance changed. She paced from one corner of the sitting room to the other without saying anything to him. Then Kokoette went and knelt before her and passionately asked for forgiveness.

Ukeme, the supposed pregnant lady was lately discovered by Kokoette to have taken advantage of his anxiety and used charades to sustain a relationship with him without any trace of pregnancy. She had left Kokoette's place back to her family residence for two days without telling him. Then Kokoette went to see her at her place. The door was left ajar and Ukeme sat at a corner talking noisily and happily with a friend how she had left Kokoette's place so he would not notice her menstrual flow and finally come to the knowledge that she was not pregnant. Without noticing Kokoette's presence, who all the while stood listening to her, she excitedly declared how Kokoette threw his wife out of the house after beating her, just because she told him she was pregnant for him. kokoette had enough, hence he silently left Ukeme's place, still unnoticed. From Ukeme's place, he passed down to Charlotte's residence to seek reconciliation with his wife.

While still kneeling before Becky and tearfully asking for her forgiveness. Becky's phone rang and Charlotte rushed with it to the parlour to put her through with the caller. She accepted it and spoke gloomily into the phone, only to here Dr. Itoro Brain's voice. After the pleasantries and seeking to know how Becky was faring, she summarily announced that Becky was six weeks pregnant. Becky re-enquired to be sure she heard her clearly. Dr. Itoro Brain confirmed the news and there went an explosive shout of joy. Becky's illnesses and weaknesses had suddenly disappeared. Charlotte rushed back into the sitting room to hear the news and Kokoette sprung up, held his wife and passionately kissed every part of her face without remembering she had not formally forgiven him or approved their re-union. The news connected everything and mended all ruptured places of their marriage. After thanking Charlotte for her outstanding kindness, Kokoette left with his wife, Becky to their marital home.

Ekemini Chad, Charlotte's husband suddenly became restless because of Charlotte's absence. It was as if something invisibly controlled the operation of his emotions. He went to his office and tried to work, but could not. The pressure of staying without his dear wife suddenly dawned on him. His thoughts could not but linger around the good times they had together and the blessedness of having her around him. Then all of a sudden, he discovered the new woman was the problem and realized just then that since he moved in with the lady, he had continued to miss his wife. He began to call Charlotte who continued to ignore his calls. This got him more anxious and restless. He suddenly realized he needed to see her face to face, hence he drove into his compound at night, a time he was sure she would be around. He went straight to the door and rang the bell. Charlotte came out, saw him and opened the door without a word. She left it ajar and went and sat at the couch. He came and stood before her and started rendering a passionate apology that was so bulky and unusual. After moments of expressing his deep remorse, Charlotte raised him up, kissed him and assured him he has been forgiven. Then she told him:

'It wasn't your fault, but mine. But everything is alright now!'

They hugged each other passionately. Then suddenly, they were at it like tiger and tigress and only struggled to locate the bedroom.

Satisfied everything had been sorted out, Alice returned to her mother's place. Two days after her return, her husband kept on calling her from London and she kept on ignoring his calls. Then he talked to Alice's mum to beg for forgiveness and begged her to help him beg Alice. For another two weeks, he called and still Alice kept on ignoring him talking to her. Then her mother spoke to her in a bid to reconcile both of them.

'No, you will talk with him this time!' Alice's mum screamed at her.' What else do you expect him to do? Any man in his situation would do the same. I know you're hurt, but at least hear him out and remember he is an African man. Now, look at me in the eyes and tell me you no longer love him and I will tell him never to call again!'

Alice stared weakly at her mother and remained silent. With this action, her mother screamed:

'You see! You still love him. Come and speak with him!'

Alice's mother put a call through to her son-in-law. Once it connected, she spoke with him and asked him to speak with his wife. Kenneth Ndudu's voice came from the other end. He was so sober and deeply remorseful. He did his rendition of apology in a tone of passion. Then Alice asked after Susan, the second wife whom he brought to replace her. He told Alice how Susan became so hostile and withdrawn immediately she had miscarriage. Then without any problem, moved out and since they were not officially married, he allowed her go.

'So what do you want now, Ken?' Alice asked.

'I want you to board the next available flight to London!' Kenneth's voice replied.

'And you think that is easy?' Alice asked.

'Please don't turn me down. I really love you. I'm already miserable without you…'

While Kenneth continued saying those things, Alice felt warm tears streamed down her cheeks and she detached the phone from her ear. Her mother noticed and asked Kenneth to call back later since she was in a bad mood.

Kenneth called back later and everything went well again between both of them. Few weeks later, Alice rejoined her husband in London.

Unaware of the new development, Ukeme walked majestically into Kokoette house, only to encounter a new reality. Kokoette ordered her out of the compound and never to return. While she was trying to reconcile the strange development, Kokoette called Becky to bring the remnant of her things. When Becky appeared at the scene, Ukeme nearly fainted. Kokoette flung her things at her with thousands of derogatory names used in describing her. Then he finally ordered the caretaker to put her away and would have his job relieved of him any day she is allowed into the compound again. Ukeme left, not being able to recover from her sudden negative twist.

The days and the months drew closer than the four friends realized and expected. Their individual marital atmosphere was so charged and powered that the happiness that covered their faces was like dripping oil. At exactly nine months, Mmamma hosted and gave birth to a set of twins. The news flew round the country side how a supposed barren woman broke off all the records in the Guinness

World Book of Record. The story was on everybody's lips and the news replenished as one of the awesome miracles of the year that was duly given to men by GOD.

Almost simultaneously, Becky gave birth to a baby girl and the jubilation increased. It was becoming so unusually strange to her in-laws who proudly beat hands on their breast that Becky would die a barren woman or a woman only capable of giving birth to dead children. Here, they were terribly disappointed and Becky became the one to laugh last. Then Charlotte, after almost three months of seeing what happened to Mmamma and Becky, gave birth to a handsome baby boy. For people who knew the supposed four barren women, it was a time of great reflection on how not to conclude the present situation of a man as the finality of his earthly outcome. While they were still reflecting on the manifest power of GOD in the midst of ordinary mortals, a hot news was imported into the country that Alice had given birth to a bouncing baby girl and had concluded plans to bring her mother down to London for baby-sitting.

To show none of the births were coincidence, Mmamma gave birth to two other children; Becky to two new children; Charlotte and Alice to two each. Here, the deal became sealed and the childless women became professional counselors to childless couple. So visible it became that the harsh circumstances of their inactions refined them into something better; into a people who never gave up, but stayed in the possible outcomes of life. Although nemeses measured and met up with four of them, but the unyielding will to succeed powered them up and left them the classic four. While one needs to be careful not to incur the natural law of nemesis, one has not to give up no matter how dreaded and difficult a person's circumstance is.

www.ingramcontent.com/pod-product-compliance
Ingram Content Group UK Ltd.
Pitfield, Milton Keynes, MK11 3LW, UK
UKHW022219230426
12048UKWH00016BA/948